The Curse of Hollister House

A Cat in the Attic Mystery

by
Kathi Daley

CHAPTER 1

Sunday

When I was a little girl, I would sit with my cat high up in the attic window overlooking the lake, dreaming the dreams only little girls can imagine. I'd plot adventures and weave enchanted tales as the seasons turned and the years unwound. It was a magical time, filled with possibilities that existed only in my mind. I'd imagined fairies in the forest, mermaids in the lake, and gnomes in the garden. As a child sitting in that window, nothing had seemed impossible, but as a broken adult sitting in the same window a quarter century later, I had to admit, if only to myself, that somewhere along the way, the magic I'd once believed in, had died along with my dreams.

"Callie, are you up there in the attic?" Great-Aunt Gracie called up the stairs.

"Yes, Aunt Gracie," I called back.

"Is Alastair up there as well?"

I glanced at the black cat sitting in the window next to me. "He is."

"I'm going to run to the market to pick up something for dinner. Is there something you'd prefer?"

I'd lost my appetite about the same time I'd lost my reason for living, but I supposed I did have to eat. "Anything is fine."

"Okay, dear. I won't be long."

I pulled the cat into my lap as Gracie drove away. I ran my fingers through his long black fur as I turned slightly and looked around the room, filled with boxes and discarded furniture from generations of Hollisters. As the last Hollister daughter, I knew the house, lakefront property, private dock, and groundskeeper's cabin would one day be mine, but to be perfectly honest, I wasn't sure I wanted it.

Setting the cat on the floor, I unfolded myself from the window. I wrote my name—Calliope Rose Collins—in the dust covering one of the tables that had been stored by some previous resident. I remembered doing the same thing as a child living in this house after my parents died, and somehow, in that moment, I felt connected to that child and the dreams she'd once held in a way I hadn't in a very long time. I'd done my best to go after those dreams and bring my fantasies into reality. But along the way, I'd learned that what we plan for and what we are destined to have don't always line up.

Alastair darted under a sheet that was draped across an old sofa. I supposed if you were a cat, the attic was filled with all sorts of magical places to explore. I could hear him swatting at something beneath the covering as I wandered around the large space, opening boxes and sifting through the contents inside. When I was a child, the boxes and their contents had seemed like treasures. The old clothes left by ancestors long gone had provided hours of entertainment as I tried on each piece and let my imagination take me where it might. The old top hat had become a magician's hat, the costume jewelry a queen's dowry, and the yellowed wedding dress a ball gown. The books stored in the boxes had provided hours of escape, the old art supplies a creative outlet, and the old piano, which some ancestor had schlepped all the way up to the attic before I was even born, a window to my soul.

I'd found a safe haven in this attic. Not only had I found solace during a time when little could comfort me, but I'd also found meaning and passion for the one thing that had pierced my grief and mattered. Pausing, I turned and looked around the room, searching for the piano. I remembered the first time I'd stumbled across the fascinating device that would deliver wonderful music with the touch of a finger. I'd been enchanted from the first keystroke and had begged Gracie to teach me to play. And she had. She'd taught me the notes and how to read music, but it was the hours spent alone with the melodies that existed only in my imagination that cemented a love affair that I was sure would last a lifetime. I looked down at my hands. Using my right forefinger, I traced the long scar that ran down my left arm from elbow to wrist. I tried to move fingers that, at times, refused to cooperate. Everyone said I'd been lucky. Everyone said that it could have been so much worse. Everyone said that having a life without music was better than having no life at all.

They were wrong.

I swallowed hard and forced myself to move on. While the attic was dusty, crowded, and unorganized, I did appreciate that everyone that had lived in the house had left something of themselves behind. Even I'd left boxes of old toys and outgrown clothing when I'd moved away. I wondered why Aunt Gracie hadn't just taken all this junk to the secondhand store, but I supposed if she did, some future resident of the house would be robbed of the opportunity to play dress up and spin tales of salty pirates and kidnapped princesses the way I had.

Longing pierced my heart as I opened a box of photos. I picked up an old Polaroid of my parents on their wedding day. They looked so happy, so optimistic about the future. My mother and I looked a lot alike. Dark hair, dark eyes, a petite frame barely reaching five feet in height. My father, in contrast, had been tall and blond. His blue eyes sparkled with happiness as he stared back at the photographer. I knew I'd joined the couple and created a family just ten months after the photo had been taken, and four years after that, the people I most depended on would be forever ripped from my life.

Setting the box of photos aside, I lifted the sheet in search of the cat. "Alastair," I called.

"Meow," he responded from across the room.

I turned and tried to home in on his exact location. There were a lot of objects for something as small as a cat to hide behind, so I started across the attic in the general direction of the meow. I supposed if I didn't find him by the time Gracie returned, I'd just leave the door ajar and he'd find his own way out. I maneuvered carefully through sheet-covered furniture and dust-covered boxes, jumping involuntarily as I bumped into the dressmaker's mannequin. I remember how terrified I'd been of the lifelike shape when I'd first seen it. As a four-year-old, I'd been sure the form came to life when no one was looking. Gracie had been patient with me, taking her time to convince me that the stuffed dressmaker's tool wasn't real. It had taken several months, but eventually, I stopped screaming every time I saw the dang thing.

Aunt Gracie had always had a lot of patience. After my parents died, I felt so alone in the world, but Gracie had taken her time with me. She'd tried very hard to make me feel at home in my new surroundings, but I never really had until she'd introduced me to the attic and the magic that could be found in the little room beneath the rafters. Old houses, with their history, their lifelines, and their curses fascinated me. Despite the tragedy that seemed to be connected to my own family home, I loved the idea of longevity, and places where multiple generations shared a single space.

Pulling a sheet away from the portrait of my great-great-grandmother, Edwina Birmingham, I thought about my parents' death and considered the family curse. Apparently, Edwina had seduced Jordan Hollister away from her best friend, Hester Stinson and, in retaliation, Hester, a purported witch, had laid a curse on the happy couple that had stipulated that any Hollister daughter born to Jordan and Edwina, or any daughter born to their descendants, would suffer the tragic and early loss of their beloved. Neither Jordan nor Edwina were concerned about the curse because the couple had only one child, a son they named Samuel. Samuel married a woman named Anastasia, who he brought to live at Hollister House. Anastasia gave birth to twin daughters, Gwendolyn and Gracie.

Gracie, the younger of the twins, continued to live in the house but never married or had children. Gwendolyn moved to Denver, where she married a man named Richard Hastings. Richard fell to his death on the couple's one-year anniversary, so Gwendolyn, who was pregnant with twins at the time of her husband's death, moved home, where she delivered Phoebe and Penelope. On the twins' second birthday, Gwendolyn died of a broken heart, leaving Gracie to raise her nieces.

Penelope never married or had children. She loved to travel and never seemed to stay put until an unfortunate encounter with a French artist, a hot Ferrari, and an ill-advised joy ride ended in her death on a narrow country road just outside Paris.

My mother, Phoebe, unlike her twin, was the sort to settle in and plant roots. She married a man named Roderick Collins. Ten months after marrying, they had a daughter, me, and four years after that, Roderick and Phoebe were killed in an automobile accident. I supposed there were those who would argue that the tragic yet unrelated deaths of three Hollister women over five generations didn't constitute the results of a curse, and perhaps they'd be right. But I also knew that things like curses weren't to be trifled with. I was now the only Hollister offspring alive and of childbearing age to carry on the curse, if one existed. Whether or not the curse was real didn't really matter; even if it was, I knew it would end with me.

Picking up the cat, I headed for the door. The dust in the attic was beginning to irritate my sinuses, so perhaps a walk out by the lake would help. I set Alastair on the floor after closing the door behind me and headed down the stairs. Stepping out of the house onto the lawn that grew from the edge of the front porch down to the waterline, I stood and watched the sun as it dipped toward the horizon. I placed a foot onto the garden path that led down to the dock. Gracie loved her garden. She'd always said her prizewinning flowers filled the space in her soul left by the children she'd never had. The winters were harsh here in the Colorado Rockies, but every spring Gracie coaxed her garden back to life, and every winter she tucked it in beneath a scattering of hay to protect the delicate plants.

After walking down the path lined with flowers in warm fall colors, I stood at the water's edge. I closed my eyes and listened as the frogs, with their long-drawn-out calls, competed with the buzz created by insects hovering over the crystal-clear water. I thought of the lush gardens and magical fairyland I'd played in as a child. I thought of the wraparound deck where I'd rocked in the swing with Gracie's cat, Archie, as I'd shared with him my hopes and dreams. When I'd left, I hadn't planned to return to Foxtail Lake. I'd believed the answers to my dreams lay elsewhere. I couldn't wait to leave the sleepy small town behind, but I had to admit I'd been happy here once. Perhaps with enough time, I'd find the peace and solace I longed for within the walls of the Hollister family home, the way I'd found peace and solace within those same walls after my parents' death.

Taking a deep breath, I lifted my face to the setting sun and allowed the warm evening air to wrap me in a warm hug. I had no idea what I was going to do with my life now that the career I'd poured my entire being into had come abruptly to an end. I'd worked so hard to get where I'd been, only to have it stripped from my hands by a drunk driver who never should have been on the road in the first place. While Gracie had taught me to understand the keys and play simple songs, the years of relentless focus and practice had helped me to perfect my gift until I'd managed to get it just right. By the time I'd graduated high school, I'd wanted nothing more than to focus on my music. Sharing the music in my soul with auditoriums filled with people who loved my melodies almost as much as I might seem like a lofty goal, but it was a dream I'd worked hard for, and had realized by my twenty-fourth birthday. It hadn't been an easy life, and the hours of practice were long, but oh, how I'd loved traveling to interesting places and meeting new people. I'd had a good life, a meaningful and complete life. Until…

I tried once again to flex the fingers on my left hand. I could move them, but the movements were slow and the range of motion limited. My doctor said that with a lot of hard work, maybe I'd regain the full use of the hand, but I knew in my soul that I'd never again have a chance to play at Carnegie Hall.

I blew out a breath, closed my eyes, and tried to refocus my mind. I knew that obsessing over what had happened would get me nowhere. Life, I'd decided, was cruel and unfair, but what was done was done, and nothing I could do would bring the music back to me. I opened my eyes and looked around at the peaceful setting. Glancing toward the caretaker's cabin, I thought about Mr. Walden. He'd lived on the property since before I'd come to live here as a child. Gracie hadn't mentioned him since I'd come slumping home with my tail between my legs two days ago, which made me wonder if he still lived on the property, or even if he was still alive. This was the first time I'd ventured from the house, so I supposed he might be around and I just hadn't noticed.

I was about to head back inside when I heard sirens in the distance. That sound always transported me back to the accident in which my parents had died, but I'd escaped with only minor injuries. I'd been told that being strapped in a car seat in the back seat had made all the difference, but there had been many occasions in those first painful years when I wasn't certain that surviving had been a good thing.

"Quite the ruckus going on across the lake."

I turned and smiled. "Mr. Walden." I hugged the grizzly old man whose skin was a sort of leathery brown after a lifetime in the sun.

"I guess now that you're all grown up, you can call me Tom."

"Okay. Tom. How are you? I was wondering if you still lived on the property."

"I'm fine. Been a while."

I nodded. "It has. I know I should have come back for a visit sooner, but you know how it is." I turned back toward the lake. The flash of lights from emergency vehicles could be seen against the darkening sky. "I wonder what's going on."

"I heard on the scanner that a body was found near the campground."

I narrowed my gaze. "I'm sorry to hear that. Do you know what happened?"

"There was talk of a bear. I guess we'll see. The last time there was a bear attack, it didn't turn out to be a bear at all."

"Like with Stella."

"Exactly like with Stella," Tom agreed.

Stella Steinmetz had been my best friend when I was in junior high. She'd disappeared while walking home from school one day. There were no clues to what had happened to her until her body was found weeks later in an unmarked grave. It appeared that she'd been attacked by a vicious animal, most likely a bear, but we all know that bears don't bury their prey.

At the time of Stella's disappearance, I'd been devastated. Not only had she been my best friend, but the only reason she'd been walking alone, and probably the only reason she was attacked, was because we'd argued and I'd left school without waiting for her as I usually did. Yes, I was only twelve at the time, and I realize now, after years of counseling, that twelve-year-old friends tend to have spats, and I'd almost let the therapist convince me that her death wasn't my fault, but there hadn't been a day since Stella's body was found that I hadn't wished I'd done things differently.

They never did figure out who'd attacked her or why her face had been shredded the way it had been. They never figured out who had robbed a young girl

"Gracie mentioned that you were going to have to take a break from performing while your hand heals. You know how much Ned and I care about you. We've both been praying for you."

I swallowed hard. "Thank you. I appreciate that. And I'm not simply taking some time off from my career." I looked down at my hand. "I'm afraid my career is pretty much over."

Nora patted my arm. "I'm so sorry, dear. I know how much your music meant to you. Do you have any idea what you might do next?"

"I'm not sure. I've been offered a teaching opportunity in New York, but I felt like I needed some time to think things through before deciding."

"I don't blame you one bit. Taking some time for a bit of peace and quiet away from the hustle and bustle of the big city will be just the thing. I've only visited New York once, but I found the noise from the traffic and whatnot to be so overwhelming that I couldn't think straight there."

"You get used to the noise once you are there for a while. In fact, it is almost comforting. Being back at Foxtail Lake where it is so completely quiet at night has made it hard to sleep."

Nora chuckled. "I guess there are those who like the quiet and those who don't. You always did seem to gravitate toward the big city." Nora hugged me again, almost smothering me to her ample bosom. "Gosh, I'm glad to have you back." Nora looked toward the door that led to a short hallway that I knew led to the back room. "Ned," she called loudly. "Come on out here and say hi to Callie."

I spent the next twenty minutes catching up with Ned and Nora and everyone who came into the store who I'd known from before. I'd been away for fourteen years, so in a way, it was amazing to me how quickly I began to feel like I'd never left. I supposed that was the way things were in the small town of Foxtail Lake. Those who left seemed to go right out of high school, but those who stayed tended to stay for a lifetime. I never thought I'd be one of the ones to stay, but I had to admit there was something comforting about being in the midst of people who knew you way back when.

"I guess you heard that Cass has a suspect in custody who he has reason to believe might be responsible for Tracy Porter's death," a woman named Lettie Harper informed the group who'd gathered to welcome me home.

Ah, the fearful whispering I'd been expecting.

"I hadn't heard," Ned, a tall, thin man answered, leaning in and lowering his voice just a bit. "Do you know who it is?"

"A drifter who has been staying in the campgrounds where Tracy's body was found. I can't say that I caught his name, but from what I understand, the guy has several arrests for vagrancy and that sort of thing."

I frowned. "That doesn't seem right. If this man who was just passing through killed Tracy, her death wouldn't be linked to Stella's. Given the fact that both girls appeared to have been mauled, and both were found buried in shallow graves, it seems to me there is a link that should be looked at, at the very least."

Lettie shrugged. "I guess Cass might have considered the fact that Tracy's death is similar to Stella's. I suppose you'll have to ask him if he found evidence that the two aren't related. He's been around for as long as anyone, so I would think the similarities would have stood out to him. Maybe he has a reason for suspecting this drifter."

"Maybe," I said, all the while thinking that perhaps it was time to stop by the sheriff's office to let Cass know I was home.

"I heard they are going to close the school for a week or so," Ned offered. "Folks are scared to let their children out of their sight."

"Seems to me the time to have closed the school would have been after Tracy went missing. If the killer planned to take another child, it makes sense that he would have done so right away, not wait until the body was found," Lettie added.

"If you ask me, there needs to be better monitoring of the kids who walk to and from school," Nettie said. "It's a different world out there nowadays. I'm afraid the days of leaving your doors unlocked and your windows open have come to an end."

As the group spoke, I could almost see the dark cloud of fear growing and expanding. Based on what had happened in the past, I knew the fear would spread like an infectious disease until the entire community was strangled by the darkness. I'd had enough darkness in my life lately and was about to excuse myself and move on when the conversation seemed to drift toward the upcoming Harvest Festival, which was held during the last weekend in October. I felt the dark cloud dissipate just a bit as I remembered how much fun the event had been when I was a child.

Every year a traveling carnival rolled into town and set up in the field on the edge of the park. The town used the event as a fund-raiser and offered hayrides, pumpkin carving, a kiddie carnival and maze, and even a haunted barn. I wasn't sure the event was set up exactly the same now, but I found I was almost as excited to find out as I had been when I was a kid. Riding the tilt-a-whirl or eating corn dogs drizzled with mustard had not been the sort of thing that had been part of my life for a very long time. When I'd left Foxtail Lake, I'd been eager to shed my small-town upbringing, so hanging out down by the lake and attending community events had become a thing of the past. As an adult, I'd set aside any fun I might otherwise have had in favor of long hours practicing the piano in pursuit of my dream.

After leaving the general store, I headed down Main toward the sheriff's office. I couldn't be certain that Cass would be in, or that he'd have time to speak to me even if he was, but I figured it didn't hurt to pop in and see what happened. Looking back, I really wasn't sure why Cass and I had drifted apart. We'd been friends since the first grade, and we'd become even closer after Stella died. When I left for New York, we vowed to stay in touch, and we had, for a while, but at some point, our daily phone conversations turned into weekly ones, and then monthly texts, before fading away completely.

I liked to think I was the cool and sophisticated sort, having lived and worked in the Big Apple and survived. Well, at least I'd survived until recently, but as I approached the local sheriff's office, I couldn't help but notice that my heart rate had quickened and my hands had begun to sweat. Cass and I had been friends for a long time, and I had no reason to believe that anything had changed, but I still couldn't help but feel nervous. The interior of the old brick building was both dark and cool. I didn't recognize the woman sitting behind the counter, so I introduced myself and asked if Deputy Wylander was in. She smiled politely and told me to take a seat, and she would see if he was available. I did as instructed, but I couldn't help but notice the territorial look she sent me when asking me to wait. If this woman thought I was somehow a threat to whatever she had going on with Cass, she was dead wrong. When it came to romance, I wasn't interested in that sort of a relationship with anyone.

Looking around the room, I had to admit the place looked cleaner and a lot more organized than it was the last time I'd been here. The Foxtail Lake Sheriff's Office was a satellite, usually housing three or four deputies. The sheriff had his office about sixty miles away in the county seat and rarely made an appearance in our little town, preferring to let whichever deputy was presently in charge run the small office up on the mountain. When Deputy Quinby had been in charge, the little place was shabby and cluttered, but it looked as if Cass had not only cleaned things up but had put a coat of paint on the walls as well.

"Callie." Cass opened his arms to me when he walked into the room, bringing a scowl to the face of his receptionist. "I heard you were back. I've been meaning to get out to your aunt's to say hi, but things have been busy."

"I heard about the murder," I said, getting right to the point. "In fact, I wanted to talk to you about that. If you have a few minutes, that is."

Cass smiled. "I always have a few minutes for you." He turned to the woman who'd greeted me. "I'll be in my office and don't want to be disturbed unless it is a real emergency."

"Sure." She shrugged nonchalantly. "Whatever you say."

"I'm going to assume that you and the woman in the reception area are an item." I said after Cass indicated I should have a seat across from him.

"Gwen. Her name is Gwen, and no, we aren't an item," Cass denied. "We did go out a couple of times, which was a mistake, but that was it. It was all very casual."

"Are you sure she knows you aren't dating? She gave me a territorial glare and exposed her claws the minute I walked in the door and introduced myself."

Cass frowned, creating a crease between his heavy brows. "I guess I might need to have a talk with her. Later. Right now, I want to hear about you. I heard what happened. I'm so very, very sorry."

"Honestly, I don't want to talk about me or the accident that ended my career. At least not right now. Maybe we can catch up sometime when you're off-duty."

"I still volunteer at the shelter twice a week. Maybe you want to come with me, like old times."

"I'd love to." When Cass and I were in high school, one of the requirements for graduation was doing community service. Cass and I had decided to volunteer at the local animal shelter. The director of the then country run facility needed help exercising the animals, so two afternoons a week he and I and a third classmate named Naomi Potter, would show up and take out as many dogs as we had time to walk.

That had been a long time ago, and things had changed. I was sort of surprised Cass was still doing it. "When do you volunteer?"

Cass relaxed back into his chair. It seemed obvious to me that he enjoyed working with the animals as much as he always had. "Tuesday and Friday afternoons when I can. If you want to meet me there tomorrow at four o'clock, we can walk the dogs and catch up at the same time."

"I'll be there."

"Great. Do you know where Naomi moved once she took the shelter private?"

"The old Johnson farm." Aunt Gracie had told me that Naomi had not only stayed on with the shelter but had taken it over and privatized it.

"That's right." Cass shuffled some of the paperwork on his desk. I couldn't help but notice that the tension around his eyes had returned. "So, you are here to discuss the Tracy Porter case."

I nodded. "I'm sure you must realize how eerily similar her murder is to Stella's."

Cass looked me in the eye. "I do realize that, and no, I don't think the man I have in custody is actually the one who killed Tracy. To be honest, the whole thing is just too neat. In my experience, if someone is going to go to all the trouble to kidnap a young girl and then kill her in a violent and unusual manner, he isn't going to be so sloppy as to leave a load of evidence behind."

"So why arrest the guy if you don't think he's guilty?"

"The problem I'm faced with is that physical evidence was found at the burial site that links to Buck Darwin. Buck has been hanging around since before Tracy went missing, and when I interviewed him about the items, he was either unable or unwilling to provide an explanation for where he was at the time Tracy was believed to have been abducted, or why things like a T-shirt with his DNA on it was found so close to the location of her temporary grave. I know the evidence suggests that Darwin is our guy, and while I normally am one to follow the evidence to its natural end, in this case, I believe it may have been planted. I told the sheriff that I didn't think Darwin was the one despite the evidence, but he is being pressured by the mayor to make an arrest, and so far I can't prove Darwin *wasn't* involved in Tracy's death, so I had no choice but to bring him in."

"I see. Doesn't whoever is mayor now want you to find the real killer?"

Cass ran a hand through his thick dark hair. I could see the pain and indecision in his eyes. "Frank White is the current mayor, and he just wants the case closed. The entire community just wants the case closed. People are scared, and the consensus is that people will continue to be scared until the killer is behind bars."

"I don't really get that line of reasoning, because having the wrong person behind bars shouldn't make anyone feel safe, but I guess I understand why you arrested the guy. Are you still digging around, or is the real killer going to get off scot-free?"

"I'm still digging around, but Mayor White has already issued a press release telling everyone that Tracy's killer has been found. Based on all the speculation and gossip going around, I don't think anyone believes that, but White is sticking to the story."

"That's crazy."

"Maybe, but there are folks in a position to make my life miserable who don't want me to continue to investigate the murder, so I'm being forced to tread lightly. The mayor has only been in town for a few years, and the sheriff just transferred from the Denver office six years ago. Neither man was here when Stella died. If they had been, they might think differently."

I felt my stomach churn at the memory of what had happened to Stella. I remembered her smile and the way she'd always known exactly what to say when I was feeling down. I didn't even remember what we'd argued about that caused her to walk home alone that day, but the odds were it had been my fault. Even I had to admit I'd been a testy kid, with strong opinions and very little patience. Most of the arguments I'd entered into had originated with me. "We need to get this guy. The real killer. For Stella. We need to make him pay for what he did back then and, apparently, what he is continuing to do."

"We will. One way or another, we will."

CHAPTER 3

Tuesday

As I've already mentioned, a woman named Naomi Potter runs the Foxtail Lake Animal Shelter. And as I've also mentioned, Naomi went to the same high school as Cass and me, and had, along with us, done her community service at the county shelter. Naomi had a tender heart and couldn't bear to see unwanted animals euthanized, so she started taking dogs and cats who could not otherwise be placed into her home. According to Cass, she'd started out small, but as word got out about her willingness to shelter strays and no longer wanted pets, she'd needed more space, so she sold her home in town and purchased fifty acres with both a house and a barn just outside the town limits. Over the years, she'd added large animal pens, a heated kennel, and well-equipped indoor and outdoor play areas. She'd even added a shallow pond for the dogs to splash around in during the hot summer months. Cass had indicated that Naomi's goal was to match as many of the animals in her charge with loving humans as possible, but it was clear it was also her goal to make them as comfortable as possible while they waited for those new homes.

"Callie!" Naomi greeted me with a hug. "I was so happy to hear that you were home. It's been a while." She pulled back slightly, her blue eyes boring into mine. "You look great. Really great. And I love your hair. I always knew you'd look good with bangs."

"You look fantastic as well." I smiled at the petite woman who'd grown leaner and stronger with years of physical labor. Her long blond hair was pulled back in a braid and the golden tan she sported from hours outdoors negated the need for makeup. I looked around the area surrounding the pasture, where I'd found Naomi tending to several small mules. "It looks like you've really built yourself something fantastic here."

"The animals are my passion, and I've worked hard to do what I can to save as many as possible. Cass may have already told you this, but I started off by taking hard-to-place animals into my home, but once word got out that I provided a home-away-from-home for shelter animals, everyone began bringing them to me. The kill shelter in the next town over officially closed their doors two years ago after everyone stopped taking their discarded animals to them, which I consider to be one of my more significant victories."

"That's wonderful. I am really happy to hear that. Cass told me he volunteers here and I'd like to do so as well, at least for as long as I am in town."

"And how long will that be?"

"I'm not sure. A while at least."

"Well, I'm happy to have you for as long as you are in the area." She took my arm and began to walk me toward the small house where she lived.

"I noticed that you have an obstacle course set up behind the house."

"In addition to running the shelter, I also offer dog training," Naomi informed me. "A well-trained dog is a lot more likely to find a wonderful forever home than a dog with behavior problems. All my charges undergo a beginner's class. My best students are provided with advanced classes, which is where the obstacle course comes in."

"That's really great." I hugged Naomi's arm. "I mean it. I know you and me and Cass volunteered for the shelter in the beginning to meet our community service requirement, but you have definitely gone the extra mile."

Naomi indicated that I should take a seat at the outdoor table on her covered porch. Two lab puppies wandered over to say hi after she went into the house to fetch us each a glass of iced tea. I bent down to scratch the two rambunctious dogs behind the ears. Growing up in Hollister House, I'd never had a dog. Gracie had had several cats over the years, but for some reason every time I brought up the idea of a puppy, she changed the subject. I supposed the world was made up of dog people and cat people. Gracie was most definitely a cat person. I can't say as I was either exactly. I enjoyed the cats who lived in the house over the years, but they were Gracie's cats, not mine. After I left Gracie's home, I'd been too busy to have a pet of any sort. I wasn't sure why Cass and I had settled on the animal shelter as our community service project, but the odds were, Cass had wanted to spend time with the dogs, and I'd wanted to spend time with Cass.

"There was a message from Cass on my machine," Naomi informed me after handing me a tall glass of iced tea. "He is running a little late but will be here shortly." She looked toward the sky. "Of course, with the short days, it might be dark before you even get started. I suppose you could take a group into the indoor play area. The dogs don't care if they are taken off the property. All they really care about is getting attention from the humans who come to spend time with them."

"How many animals do you have here?" I asked.

"Currently, forty-two dogs, six puppies, seventeen cats plus two litters of kittens, five mules, four rabbits, an old dairy cow that I've officially retired to my closest pasture, two horses I'm still hoping to place, and a llama with an ornery disposition named Harry, who I'm pretty sure is here to stay."

"Wow. It must take you all day just to feed and clean up after so many animals."

"It's a project, that's for sure, but I have a volunteer staff who help out a lot. Some of my volunteers help with feeding and cleaning, while others prefer to spend time playing with the animals. I even have someone who handles my bookkeeping.

This place runs off donations, so I am careful to keep clean records. So, tell me what you've been up to since you left Foxtail Lake."

"Not a lot," I answered vaguely. "I left Foxtail Lake to focus on my music. Once I became established, I did some tours overseas, as well as a few concerts in the States. I'd just been booked into Carnegie Hall when I was in an auto accident that damaged the nerves in my left hand, so here I am, back in Foxtail Lake where it all began."

Naomi gave me a look that assured me that she knew my life story couldn't be boiled down to a couple of sentences. I knew that she was interested in the details, but I wasn't quite ready to talk about them, so I asked her about the golden aspens that were planted all up and down the road leading from her property to the main road. They were in full color at this time of the year and simply stunning. There had been some color in New York, not that I'd taken the time to notice, but fall in Colorado could not be outdone.

Naomi must have decided to let me avoid the topic I'd made it clear I didn't want to discuss and began telling me about the fall garden she'd planted. She offered to show it to me, and we'd both just stood up when Cass pulled onto the shelter road. Deciding to wait for a tour of the garden, Naomi and I headed toward the driveway.

"I'm sorry I'm late," Cass said when he'd climbed out of his sheriff's department SUV.

"It's not a problem," Naomi said. "It was nice to have a chance to catch up with Callie. It's been a while."

"Too long," Cass agreed.

I was beginning to feel weird about the fact that Cass and Naomi were talking about me as if I wasn't there, so I jumped in and asked about the dog looking out the back window of Cass's vehicle.

He turned and looked at the huge German shepherd. "That is Milo. He's been with me a little over two years and, quite frankly, he is the best partner I've ever had."

"He's beautiful. I don't suppose he will be allowed to get out and play with the other dogs."

Cass opened the tailgate and called the dog over to where he was standing at the corner of the vehicle. He took off his vest and replaced the harness he wore with a regular dog collar. "Milo is off-duty now, so he can join us." Cass stepped aside, and the dog jumped out of the back. He made a beeline for Naomi, who greeted him with a hug.

"So I take it he knows that when he is wearing his harness he is on duty, and when he is wearing the red collar you replaced it with he is off-duty."

Cass nodded. "Basically. When he is on duty, we don't encourage social interaction with other dogs or people outside his team on the force, but when he is off-duty, he plays and cuddles just like any other dog."

Once Naomi had a chance to greet Milo, Cass called him over and introduced him to me. I tentatively reached out and scratched the dog's massive neck. I swore he smiled at me. "He's really great. Does he go home with you?"

"He not only goes home with me but he sleeps in my bed." Cass looked toward the darkening sky. "I guess it is too late to walk the dogs."

"I'd just suggested to Callie that we bring a few dogs into the indoor play area. They won't mind if they miss their walk as long as they have plenty of human interaction."

Cass agreed to the plan, so Naomi went to fetch the dogs we would play with while Cass and I went to find plenty of balls and ropes to toss.

"So, how is the investigation going?" I asked as we filled a bag with toys from the large box where Naomi kept them.

"I feel like the whole process has been stalled by the evidence against Buck, but I'm running some tests on my own to see if I can find evidence of DNA other than Buck's on the T-shirt that was found near the gravesite. If Buck was setup, as I believe he was, I'm hoping whoever planted the shirt left something else behind."

"Is Buck even trying to defend himself? It seems that if he was innocent, he would be hollering about being locked up."

"He isn't saying a thing. He hasn't admitted to the killing, but he isn't claiming to be innocent either. I'm really not sure why he would be so complacent unless someone is either threatening him or bribing him to keep him quiet."

Naomi entered the play area with ten dogs of various sizes trailing along behind her. Milo looked at Cass with hope in his eye. Cass said a word in a deep, guttural tone that sounded like it might have been German or a variation of it, and Milo took off to greet the others. It was nice to see that although he was obviously a well-trained law officer, he was able to play like a regular dog. Cass and I greeted the canines who came over to say hi. Once we'd said our hellos, we began tossing rope toys and balls for the dogs to chase.

Once we'd spent some time tossing items for the dogs to fetch, we got down on the floor to pet and cuddle those who would let us. Our ninety-minute session flew by, and by the time we were ready to leave, the dogs were exhausted, and so were we.

"Thanks again for coming by," Naomi said. "Both of you. The dogs can never really have too much people time."

"It's always a pleasure," Cass said in response.

"It really was fun," I answered. "And I'm happy to come back on a regular basis. Whenever you need me. I don't seem to have any other commitments at the moment."

"I'll look at the volunteer schedule and call you with some dates and times," Naomi promised.

"I'm picking up a pizza and heading home if you want to join me," Cass said as he lowered his tailgate and Milo jumped in.

"I'd like that, but I told Aunt Gracie I'd be home and she said she'd make a meatloaf. Rain check? If we can plan it in advance, I can let her know I won't be home for dinner, which will save her the trouble of making it."

"How about Friday? We can do a volunteer stint here at the shelter and then drop Milo off at my place and maybe go out after that."

"Sounds good, as long as we go somewhere casual. If we play with the dogs first, I'll most likely have on jeans and a sweatshirt, both of which could very well be covered in dog hair."

"You make a good point. How about tomorrow for dinner? I am usually off at five. I can head home and change and then pick you up at the lake house. There is a new steak house over on the east shore that is really very good."

"That sounds perfect. I'll see you then."

After Cass pulled away, I slipped into my own car and headed home. When I arrived, Aunt Gracie had meatloaf, baked potatoes, and green beans ready to serve. I wasn't sure how she ate when I wasn't around, but the entire time I'd been growing up and every night since I'd been back, she'd taken the time to make real food in comparison to the microwave meals I'd made when I lived in New York.

I glanced at the table, which had three place settings. "Is Tom joining us?"

"He is. I hope that is okay. It has just been Tom and me all these years, so it made sense that he would join me for a meal each evening."

"I think that is a wonderful idea. Tom has always been one of my favorite people. When I was a kid, we would sit out on the dock, and he would tell me wonderful stories about Foxtail Lake and the people who'd lived here over the years."

"He really is a very nice man, and we do enjoy each other's company. Most nights we watch television or play a game after we eat supper. Neither of us ever married or had a family, I have to say, my life would have been a lot emptier without him coming around in the evenings."

"I'm glad you had him. I'm glad we both did."

"So, how'd it go at Naomi's place?" Gracie asked as she placed hot rolls in a basket.

"It went well. She's really built an impressive facility. When Cass and I used to volunteer at the old county-run shelter, it was so depressing, but I think the animals in Naomi's care will have a good life whether they are adopted or not."

"She is an exceptional woman. Did Cass bring Milo along?"

I grabbed a stack of napkins and began setting them around the table. "He did. What a beautiful dog. And he's so smart. Cass mentioned that he made an excellent partner, and after watching him for just over an hour, I can see that he probably is. I'm not sure he can help Cass with the strategizing, but I'd want to have him by my side if I came face-to-face with a bad guy with a gun."

"Speaking of bad guys," Gracie said as she handed me a pitcher of water and asked me to pour it into the glasses she had already set out. "I had to run into town to pick up a few things, and I saw Ida Cunningham." Ida ran the local inn with her sister, Maude. Neither of the women, who must be well into their sixties now, had ever married or had children, like Aunt Gracie and Tom. "She told me that she'd heard from one of her vendors that the sheriff let it slip that he had evidence he wasn't making public regarding Tracy's murder. Now, we both know that poor old man from the campground didn't kill that child, yet as far as I can tell, the sheriff has all but closed the case. If he has evidence that he is not sharing, I think the folks who live in this town ought to call him on it."

"Cass said that the mayor is putting pressure on the sheriff to get the case closed. The man they arrested isn't helping the matter. So far, he isn't defending himself. Cass thinks he is being bribed or threatened by the real killer." I set the half-full pitcher of water on the counter after filling the glasses on the table. "Cass made it sound as if part of the problem is that they don't have evidence other than what implicates Buck Darwin. If Ida is right and the sheriff is sitting on evidence, I'm not sure that even Cass knows about it."

Gracie glanced out the window and waved at Tom Walden, who was walking toward the main house from his little cabin. "Ida might not have her facts straight. A good amount of the time she doesn't. But it might not hurt to mention the idea of suppressed evidence to Cass. If nothing else, he can do some digging around."

"Actually, I'm having dinner with Cass tomorrow. I was going to let you know so you didn't bother to make a big meal, thinking I'd be here."

"That will work out well for me. Wednesday is bingo night at the church. I usually grab a meal with some of my friends before we head over."

"That sounds like fun. I'll keep that in mind for future Wednesdays. I don't want you to change up your regular routine at all just because I'm here. I might be here for a while, so don't think of me as a guest who needs to be attended to."

Tom walked in and hung up his coat on the rack. Gracie smiled at him.

"Of course, I don't think of you as a guest. This is your home. It always will be. Tom and I want you to feel right at home. Don't we, dear?"

"Absolutely." Tom kissed Gracie on the cheek and sat down at the head of the table.

I couldn't help but smile. Apparently, my hunch about the two of them hadn't been all that far off after all.

CHAPTER 4

Wednesday

Waking to find that I had absolutely nothing on my to-do list was something I would never get used to. I supposed if I was going to be staying at the lake for an extended period, that I needed to figure out a way to fill my days. I'd known exactly what every moment of every day would consist of since I was a teenager with goals and dreams still to be realized, but now that those goals and dreams were lost, all I really felt was empty.

Sitting up, I glanced out the window. The day had dawned bright and sunny, but the weather forecast indicated there was a storm brewing and we could expect it to make its way over the summit and into the little valley where Foxtail Lake was located by nightfall. I slipped out of bed and pulled on an old pair of sweats. The room was chilly, as it would be through the long winter, and while the heating system in the old house had been on its last legs since I'd lived here the first time, I knew that there was a stack of wood already split and seasoned just waiting to fill the six fireplaces that helped to heat the lake house.

Glancing out the window, I could see that Gracie was already outside tending to her garden. After brushing my teeth and running a brush through my hair, I headed downstairs and poured myself a large cup of coffee. Sitting alone in the large, farmhouse-style kitchen was not how I wanted to start my day, so I topped off my mug and wandered out into the garden. The brilliant color of the aspens and maples that tented the yard provided a colorful backdrop for the beds of flowers that had begun to fade but at one time had created a watercolor of oranges, yellows, reds, and browns.

"You're up early," I said as I approached Gracie.

She looked up, shielding her eyes from the sun. "Storms coming. It'll be a cold one at that. I wanted to get the beds tucked in for the winter before the first snow."

Tilting my head back, I looked toward the sunny blue sky. "Do you think it will snow? It seems early."

Leaning back onto her heels, she looked up into the sky as well. "It's hard to say with these mid-October storms. Some will bring snow and others rain. But the flowers are starting to die off anyway, and the forecast is for a cooler than usual end to

October, so I figured it would be best to be prepared. Tom went into town for additional hay for the beds along the water. If you aren't busy today, we could use some help getting everything covered."

"I'd be happy to help."

"I have fresh pumpkin muffins in the tin if you want a little something with that coffee," Gracie informed me.

"Thanks, but I'll stick with just coffee for now. Do you have an extra pair of gloves?"

"In the garden shed."

It actually felt good to do something physically demanding yet totally mindless. Once Tom arrived with the bales of hay he'd purchased to complete the winterization of the garden, I set to work transferring the bales to the various parts of the yard, breaking them down and then raking them over the delicate shrubs and flowers, which would die off over the winter but reappear during the longer and warmer days of spring. Gracie's garden really was a work of art. She had daffodil bulbs that bloomed early in the spring, providing the first hint that winter was finally over. Just about the time they were dying off, the summer blooms—daisies, coneflowers, and wild roses—appeared, and just when it seemed as if they were spent and the garden would lose its brilliance, along came fall flowers like chrysanthemums to close out the year. The lake itself was beautiful in all its seasons. Deep blue water sprinkled with foxtails and lilies provided homes for the various types of wildlife contained within. When I was a child, I'd swim and poke around in Gracie's old rowboat during the summer; then, come winter, it was on with the ice skates.

As the morning waned and afternoon appeared, I could feel the breeze begin to pick up. Dark clouds gathered above the summit, and the temperature seemed to drop with each passing minute. Storms that crawl into our valley, leaving a layer of snow this early in the season, tended to blow out just as quickly. Gracie was right to cover her garden, but the reality was that once the storm blew through, the snow would melt and the warmer days of Indian summer would set in for a few weeks before winter arrived for real.

"I think we've done what we can for now," Gracie said, pulling off her gloves.

"Hopefully, if it does snow, it won't be a heavy snow," Tom added, looking toward the approaching storm. "Early snow almost always brings broken branches."

I remembered from my days at the lake that a heavy snow before the last of the leaves fell for the year was likely to bring its share of destruction. "Maybe it will just rain." I leaned on the rake I was still holding. "The temperature has dropped, but I doubt it is anywhere near freezing."

"Let's hope so," Gracie said. "I guess all we can do is wait." She glanced at Tom. "Would you like to come in for some coffee?"

"I'd like that."

Gracie looked at me. "Would you care to join us?"

"I have some emails to return, and then I need to hop in the shower to get ready for my dinner with Cass. I enjoyed helping you today. I haven't worked a garden since I left for the city. It felt good to get my hands dirty."

"You seemed to do okay today." Gracie glanced at my left hand.

"I have enough feeling and movement that I am fine doing tasks such as raking. It is my fine motor skills that may never recover. Still, I guess time will tell, and I do feel like my range of motion has improved quite a bit even in the past couple of weeks."

Gracie squeezed my arm in support and then headed toward the shed with her gardening tools. I gathered up the tools closest to where I stood and followed behind her. The wind had picked up to create a steady force that caused the aspens to quake. I paused and listened to the haunting sound made by nature's symphony. I hadn't realized how much I'd missed the anticipation of an approaching storm. Sure, it rained and even snowed in New York, but when I'd lived there, I'd spent most of my time indoors, so watching the clouds roll in and the trees begin to sway really hadn't been a factor in my life.

Once we'd all made it indoors, Tom and Gracie settled around the kitchen table, and I headed upstairs. I didn't really have emails to return. Telling Gracie that was just my way of offering an excuse to give the friends some privacy. I knew Gracie was happy to have me home, but I was equally certain that my abrupt arrival had most likely put a crimp in her normal routine.

Deciding to log on to my computer anyway, I went ahead and checked my email account to find it filled with spam. I logged off there and logged on to Google. When Stella died, I'd been just twelve. I realized something horrible had happened, but I don't remember getting caught up in the details, although I could remember the fear that had settled onto the entire community, as it seemed to have now. I remembered the loss of freedom as parents began picking their kids up from school rather than letting them walk home, and late-night games of hide-and-seek had been replaced with early curfews and nights spent in front of the television rather than out with friends.

But I also remembered that after a while, the terror of Stella's death had receded into the background and life returned to normal. After a time, doors and windows were once again left open, groups of friends played outdoors well into the evening, and children began to walk in groups to and from school. The light returned to our town, and the darkness became nothing more than a distant memory to most.

When I left Foxtail Lake, I rarely thought about my friend or the terrible circumstances surrounding her death. But now… now the fear I'd suppressed for years seemed to be finding its way back into my consciousness, and I was being pulled into the death of Tracy Porter to a degree I couldn't really explain. I'd never met the girl or her family, but I supposed that the emptiness that permeated my life since the accident had left me with a lack of purpose. If I looked at my situation objectively, it was possible that obsessing about the details surrounding the death of this young girl gave me something concrete on which to focus my attention.

Realizing that I needed to jump into the shower if I was going to be ready for our dinner date when Cass arrived, I logged off and set the notes I'd made aside. Stella had been gone a long time. The odds of her and Tracy's killer being one and the same were unlikely, yet my gut told me the deaths were connected, and it was in that connection that the answer to who'd killed both girls would be found.

CHAPTER 5

The steak house Cass took me to was a rustic log building settled on the beach on the eastern shore of the lake. The music was soft, the lighting dim, and the tables covered with white cloths. The restaurant was both elegant and woodsy, which I loved, but somehow the romantic setting made our dinner out feel a lot more datelike than I'd anticipated or was comfortable with.

"This is really lovely," I said as Cass pulled out my chair.

"It's one of my favorite places to eat. Their filets are the best quality I've ever had, and their pasta dishes are even better than Antonia's," Cass said, mentioning a local favorite. "I can assure you that anything you order will be delicious, but my favorite is the Seafood Oscar."

"Sounds good."

"The scampi and the stuffed salmon are wonderful as well. Like I said," Cass laid his napkin on his lap, "you really can't go wrong."

Cass waved the waiter over and ordered a bottle of wine. I clutched the menu, hiding behind it as I tried to get my emotions under control. I seriously needed to get a grip. Cass was a friend. Just a friend. We'd been friends for years and had shared hundreds of meals. There really was no explanation for my jitters.

"Remember that time we camped out on the beach just south of here and that family of raccoons took the bathing suits we'd left on the line to dry and carried them up the tree?"

I lowered my menu and looked over the top of it at Cass for the first time since we'd sat down. I smiled. Leave it to Cass to find a way to break the ice and put me at ease with a silly memory the two of us shared. "That was pretty aggravating at the time, but looking back, it was hilarious. We had to swim in our underwear for the rest of the trip. And let's not forget about that one superfat raccoon we named Chucky. No matter how hard we tried to keep him out of the food, he found a way in."

Cass chuckled. "I have metal containers for my food when I backpack now, but back then we'd just raid the cupboard at your aunt's place or my parents' and take off at only a moment's notice."

I couldn't remember the last time I'd done anything at a moment's notice. My life as a concert pianist had been structured and disciplined. The spontaneous teen I'd once been had been shoved down into the deepest corner of my soul once the responsibilities of adulthood had set in. "Whatever happened to Toby Wallis?" I'd brought up a friend of Cass's who'd come along on many of our expeditions and adventures.

"Toby is a ranger for the National Park System. He is currently in Glacier National Park, but he recently did a stint in Yellowstone. He married Natalie Green, who, interestingly, went on to become a wildlife veterinarian."

"Really? That's awesome." I remembered Natalie as a shy but serious student who was smarter than Cass and me put together.

"Toby and Natalie appear to live an interesting life. They travel quite a bit between the parks, but they were back in Foxtail Lake over the holidays, and we hung out a bit. They seem happy."

"It would be fun to actually live in the various parks. I'm sure there is a lot more to see and experience than you can as a visitor. But wasn't Natalie dating Daniel Gray when we were in high school?"

"She was, but they broke up. Daniel still lives in Foxtail Lake. He owns the local hardware store. You should stop by. I'm sure he'd be thrilled to see you."

"I will."

Cass and I continued to catch up while we waited for our meals to arrive. It was fun to hear how everyone turned out. Having stayed in Foxtail Lake, Cass had attended all the high school reunions, so he had pretty much kept up with everyone, while I hadn't kept up with anyone.

I intentionally avoided the subject of Tracy's murder investigation. I suspected Cass was intent on avoiding it as well. Not that I wasn't totally interested, but somehow our uncomfortable date had settled into an enjoyable meal between friends, and I didn't want to do anything to ruin the mood. Cass shared some of the highlights of his life from the past fourteen years, and I did the same. Of course, I was much more interested in his stories because I knew most of the people he spoke of and was totally able to relate.

It wasn't until we were driving home that I broached the subject that had been lingering in the back of my mind the entire evening. "I've still been thinking a lot about Stella."

"Yeah. Me too."

"I feel really bad about the fact that I barely gave her a second thought after leaving Foxtail Lake, even though she was my best friend and she died a terrible death."

"You shouldn't feel bad. You'd moved on to a new life. It's natural for the people and places from your past to fade away from your mind."

"Maybe, but I feel like it is important to keep her memory alive."

Cass placed his right hand over my left and gave it a squeeze. "This is hard for you, isn't it? Being back with your memories and your past."

"It is hard. But it's nice as well. I'm not happy about the reason I'm home, but I think I needed this time to reconnect with my past. I hadn't meant to totally lose touch with everyone here at the lake, but the longer I'm here, the more I realize I had. It's been nice being around people who knew me way back when."

"Living in a small town for your entire life has its ups and downs, but in the end, I wouldn't change a single thing. I love it here. It's my home. I really can't imagine living anywhere else."

There was a time when the only thing I could think of was living somewhere else. Anywhere else. But now? Now things somehow looked different. Everything had changed, and I was a different person than I was fourteen years ago.

After Cass dropped me off, I headed up to the attic. I guess if there was one thing that hadn't changed in all these years, it was that the little room at the top of the stairs was still the place I felt most at home. When I opened the attic door, I found Alastair curled up in the window seat. Gracie's room had been dark when I passed it, so I assumed she'd gone to bed. Strange that she hadn't taken Alastair with her. I crossed the room, picked up the cat, and curled us both into the window. It crossed my mind that it was odd he was even in the room given the fact that the door had been closed, but I supposed he might have wandered in earlier and, not knowing that he was in the room, Gracie might have closed the door.

"Lots of stars out tonight," I said to the cat as I gazed out the window at the dark sky.

"Meow."

"I really missed the sky when I lived in New York," I continued out loud. "I missed watching storms approach, sunrises over the meadow, and sunsets over the lake. I missed looking up into the sky and seeing so many stars that it looked like someone had painted them there." I hugged the cat to my chest and let the sound of his purring soothe my somewhat battered soul. "Before you came to live here, Gracie had a cat named Archie, and before Archie was Tobias. Tobias was already an old cat when I came to live with Gracie and wasn't really into accompanying me on my various adventures, but Archie and I had a lot of fun together."

The cat continued to purr. I'd forgotten how relaxing the sound of a cat purring could be.

"I used to have this little pirate hat that Gracie made for me. It was cat-size, so Archie and I could play pirate and princess. We used to have so much fun together, Archie and me." I leaned back so I could get an even better view of the sky. "I really miss him. I honestly didn't even realize that until just now." I felt a catch in my throat. "I wonder if he missed me when I left."

"Meow."

"Yes, I'm sure Aunt Gracie took good care of him. She always takes good care of everyone who is entrusted to her care." I sat up a little straighter, adjusting the cat in my arms. "We used to have this blind squirrel who lived up here in the attic. Now, most folks would have killed the trespasser, but Aunt Gracie started feeding it. She'd come up here and talk to it in a really gentle voice until eventually, the squirrel would come right up to her when she called. I guess that old squirrel must be long dead by now, but it's nice to know he found a friend in Gracie during his final days."

"Meow."

"Yes, I'm sure you would have approached the presence of a blind and helpless squirrel quite differently. Most cats would have, but the first time

Archie yowled at the poor little guy, Gracie gave him a stern warning, and Archie left him alone from that point forward." I unfolded myself from the window. "I think there is a painting of the little trespasser around here somewhere. Gracie was going through her painting stage right about the same time the squirrel moved in with us."

I walked toward the back of the attic, where I'd noticed some canvases covered with tarps. I gently lifted each one, looking for the image of that old squirrel perched in the window with the pile of nuts Gracie had given him to keep him still while she sketched him.

"Here it is." I stepped aside. "His name was Oliver."

"Meow."

"Yeah, he was a scrawny little thing, but Gracie seemed to love him."

Alastair jumped up onto a pile of boxes behind me. The one on the top fell to the floor. Old ceramic mugs wrapped in newspaper from Gracie's pottery phase had been stored inside the box. I hoped nothing had broken. I picked up the first mug and unwrapped it. It seemed fine. I checked the other two on the floor as well before beginning the process of rewrapping them. It was while I was rewrapping the third mug that I noticed the headline on the page: "Missing girl mauled to death." I set the mug aside and unfolded the old newspaper. The article had been published ten years ago. Apparently, a twelve-year-old girl who lived in the little town of Rivers Bend, about thirty miles south of Foxtail Lake, had gone missing. She'd last been seen leaving the middle school she attended on foot. There had been no sign of her for almost eight weeks until a hiker and his dog had come across a partially disturbed body. It appeared the girl had been mauled.

I looked at Alastair. "No way this is a coincidence."

CHAPTER 6

Thursday

After Alastair and I had found the newspaper article in the attic, we went downstairs to my bedroom, where he curled up and went to sleep, and I logged on to my computer. I'd spent most of the overnight hours trying to get more information about the girl. I found out that her name was Hillary Martin and she, like Stella and Tracy, had been twelve years old when she went missing. And, like the others, she'd been last seen leaving school on foot but never made it home. She had also been buried in a shallow yet well-concealed grave. Her face looked as if it had claw marks on it. Hillary had been buried long enough that there had been a significant amount of decay, but according to the article, no physical evidence was found at the gravesite. I spent hours searching for follow-up articles, but as far as I could tell, her killer was never found. Once I downed a couple of pots of coffee, I'd call Cass to see what he knew about this case.

After I'd exhausted my know-how in terms of conducting a search into Hillary's kidnapping and murder, I'd turned my attention to looking into what I could find about Tracy. Because she was a local and her disappearance was recent, there was a lot more information available. I already knew that Tracy was twelve, like Stella and Hillary, when she went missing, and like the others, she'd disappeared after taking off on foot from the middle school she'd attended. All three girls had been buried in shallow but well-concealed graves and appeared to have been mauled. I had no idea what the motive for these murders might be. As far as I knew, none of the three had been sexually assaulted before they died, but what was up with the mauling? Did the killer actually think the deaths would be blamed on a bear? Doubtful.

The article mentioned that Hillary was an only child. Stella was an only child too. I didn't know if Tracy had any siblings, but I couldn't see how not having brothers or sisters could make someone the target of a killer. Still, I'd noted the similarity on the fact sheet I'd started as I surfed the web. At several points during the long hours I'd worked on my research, I had stopped to wonder why I was spending so much time on this. It certainly wasn't my job or responsibility to figure out what had happened to these girls. Yet I felt compelled to do just that. More than compelled; I felt driven. I was sure a psychologist would tell me that I was replacing my obsession with music with these cases now that the music I'd lived my life for had been stripped away from me. I was sure they'd be right. But a displaced obsession still felt better than no sense of purpose at all.

"Morning, sweetheart," Gracie said as she came in from outside. "You slept late."

"Didn't sleep well." I yawned.

"How was your date?"

"It wasn't a date, just dinner. And it was fine. We went to the steak house on the east shore. It was really nice."

Gracie placed her gardening gloves in the utility room off the kitchen. "I've eaten there a time or two. They have some wonderful options."

"I tried the scampi. It was wonderful, although," I qualified, "not as good as yours."

Gracie smiled. She poured herself a cup of coffee and then sat down at the table across from me. "So, if it wasn't a date that kept you up all night, what was it?"

I wrapped my hands around my mug. "It was Stella. Actually, it was all the girls."

"All the girls?"

"When I got home last night, I went up to the attic the way I used to after a date, and Alastair was there. We got to chatting, and the next thing I knew, I was looking for that oil painting you did of the old blind squirrel who lived in the attic. Alastair jumped onto a box of mugs and knocked it over. Don't worry;

nothing broke. But while I was checking the status of the mugs, I found an old news article about a young girl who lived in Rivers Bend. Like Stella and Tracy, she was twelve when she went missing when she left the middle school she attended, and like Stella and Tracy, she was mauled."

"That's quite a coincidence."

"It is. Too much of a coincidence. I spent most of the night looking for additional information on both Tracy and this other girl, Hillary. I'd hoped that some sort of link other than what we already knew would stand out."

Gracie took a sip from her mug. "And did you find anything?"

"Not yet, but I plan to keep looking. Did you know Tracy and her family?"

Gracie paused before answering. "I can't say that I knew Tracy. Her mother cuts hair for the Clip and Curl, and we've chatted on occasion when I was in to have my hair done. She mentioned her daughter once or twice, but I'd never spoken to her."

"And Tracy's father?"

"He works for a local plumber. I've never met him, nor do I know anything more about him."

"The article I read said that Hillary's dad was an electrician. I don't know if that is relevant, but both men worked in construction, and Stella's dad was a general contractor."

"I suppose there might be something there, although it is equally as likely that the choice of career of the victim's fathers is totally irrelevant."

"Yeah, it doesn't seem likely that's the connection, but I'm keeping a list of everything I find. You never know when some totally simple detail could turn out to be the key to figuring out what happened and why." I paused and then continued. "Do you know if Tracy had siblings?"

"She had two half brothers from her father's first marriage. They are much older, and I think both were married before Tracy was born."

"Do they live here in town?"

"No. I remember Tracy's mom mentioning that one lives in Denver and the other in Chicago." Gracie bent down and picked up Alastair, who'd been doing circle eights through her legs. "It sounds like you are investigating these murders."

"Not investigating. But the similarities between the deaths of Tracy and Hillary have captured my attention. Maybe I just need something to occupy my mind, though I do find myself somewhat compelled to look into things. I know I'm not qualified to figure this out, but I don't see that I'm hurting anyone by digging around a bit."

"Have you spoken to Cass about this?"

"Not really. I mean, I guess a little." I took a breath. "We've discussed the similarities between Stella's abduction and death and Tracy's, but I didn't find out about Hillary until after I got home last night. I thought I'd call him later to see if he knows anything about her."

Gracie stood up and placed the cat on the floor, then took her cup to the sink. "I'm glad you found something to keep you busy, but be careful. You never know when a little scratching around might dig up a hornet's nest."

"I'll be careful."

"I have my garden club meeting today, so I will be away for a few hours. I was going to stop at the market on my way home. Is there something you'd like for dinner?"

"Lasagna." It seemed that my appetite was back for the first time since the accident.

After Gracie left, I headed outside with my second cup of coffee. The storm we'd spent most of the day yesterday preparing for had never materialized. I wasn't sure if it had simply petered out or if it was late in arriving. The dark clouds over the summit seemed to indicate that the storm might still decide to rear its ugly head.

Cupping my mug in my hands, I headed across the lawn to the old dock that had been part of the property since the house was built. Gracie had several old rowboats, all of which had been stored for the winter by now. Once I arrived at the dock, I walked slowly out toward the end. When I was about halfway there, Alastair joined me.

"Looks like that storm is just waiting over the summit."

"Meow."

I sat down on the end of the dock, letting my legs and feet dangle. I'd spent many hours in this same spot when I was a kid, skipping rocks and, if Cass was around, fishing. The water was low enough so that my feet could dangle without getting wet, but come spring when the runoff was at its height, and the rivers from the summit above the lake crashed down the narrow canyons toward the valley below, sitting on the dock and keeping your feet dry wouldn't be possible.

I leaned back slightly as a flock of geese heading south for the winter flew overhead. Alastair looked up briefly but then crouched down and went back to watching for fish. Yellow aspen leaves that had fallen from the trees along the shoreline floated past on the slightly rippled surface of the water, causing him to yowl at them as they passed under the dock.

I nestled into my sweatshirt as the cold breeze blowing down from the summit began to pick up. I wasn't sure this storm would bring snow, but there was no doubt in my mind that snow was just around the corner. As I leaned back and looked up into the darkening sky, I remembered sitting on this very dock watching other storms approach.

"Can I sit with you?"

I whirled around at the sound of a child's voice.

"I'm sorry. You startled me. I didn't hear you walk up."

"I'm Paisley. I live in the big house in the cove just around the bend."

"Nice to meet you, Paisley. My name is Callie."

"I know who you are. Gracie talks about her famous niece all the time."

"You know Gracie?"

"Sure. I come to visit, and we sit and talk. Can I sit with you?"

I moved to the left just a bit to make room. "Sure. Have a seat."

The girl sat down, and the cat climbed into her lap.

"It seems Alastair likes you," I commented.

"We're friends. My grandma is allergic, so I can't have a cat, but Gracie doesn't mind if I come to visit hers."

I tucked my legs up under my body. "You live with your grandmother?"

The girl nodded. "My mom is sick and can't take care of us, so we live with Grandma."

"And your dad?"

She shrugged. "I never met him."

"I'm sorry. I hope your mom feels better soon."

When she didn't respond, I asked her if she was here to stay.

She shrugged. "I guess so. At first, I didn't want to be here. I missed my friends, and there are no other kids living out here at the lake. But then I met Gracie and Alastair and they invited me to come to visit. I guess they are my new friends." Paisley paused and looked at me. "Gracie told me that you grew up here in the lake house. Were there other kids back then?"

"No. I mean sure, there were other kids who lived in town, but not out here at the lake. There were kids around during the summer when the campground was full, but during the winter, it was just me and Aunt Gracie, and of course Mr. Walden." I tucked a lock of hair that had blown loose from my hair tie behind my ear.

Paisley pulled Alastair closer to her chest. The poor cat didn't look all that comfortable, but he didn't struggle to be let go either.

"Gracie said that you used to spend a lot of time up in her attic playing the piano."

I nodded. "That's true. I did spend a lot of time in the attic playing the piano, and it did help me feel less lonely."

"Gracie said that maybe something like that would help me feel less lonely. Grandma doesn't have a piano, but Gracie said I could come over and use hers. She said she has two: an old one in the attic and a newer one in her living room she bought after you started playing."

"She does have two pianos, and I agree that music can be a wonderful companion."

"That's what Gracie said." Paisley adjusted her position just a bit. "I don't know how to play. Maybe you can teach me. If you aren't too busy, that is."

Suddenly, my throat constricted, and my heart began to race. I hadn't played a single note since the accident. I knew that my limitations would envelop and overwhelm me if I tried to play again. It was best to walk away and leave the past behind.

"I'm not sure how long I'll be here, but Gracie taught me, so maybe she can teach you."

The girl hung her head. Her smile faded, and she appeared to be totally crushed. "That's okay, I know you must be busy." She stood up and set the cat down on the dock. "I should go. It was nice to meet you."

I felt like the biggest loser in the world as the child walked away, but what could I do? I didn't want to seem cruel or uncaring, but at this point in my life, I was pretty sure I'd never touch a piano again.

"Don't look at me that way," I said to the cat, who actually did seem to be glaring. "You know I can't teach that girl to play. Maybe I can talk to Gracie about another idea for the two of us. Maybe Paisley would like to play dress-up the way I used to."

"Meow."

"Yes, I know I'm a coward, but I'm doing the best I can, and I don't need you rubbing it in."

I stood up, turned, and headed toward the house. I'd already dawdled away half the day. Crying over what could have been and should have been was not going to get me anywhere, yet thinking about my career made me want to curl in a ball and die, so instead I'd focus on solving the deaths of three young girls and leave the hard work I'd need to do to get on with my life for another day.

CHAPTER 7

Friday

I'd spent most of the previous afternoon digging around on the internet, trying to find out what else I could about Hillary and Tracy. I knew in my gut that their deaths had to somehow be related to Stella's; I just didn't know how. All three girls had been twelve, all had been walking home from school when they were abducted, all three had fathers who worked in the construction trade, and all were either only children or at least the only child living at home. The only-child thing seemed like a stretch, and I doubted it was relevant, but having several similarities rather than just a few made it seem more like a list.

After looking over everything I could find, I realized that I was going to need help. Professional help. Cass was already working on Tracy's murder, so it wouldn't be all that much of a stretch to talk to him about the other two murders as well. He had known Stella, same as me. He must want to find her killer as badly as I did, even after all this time. That would have seemed an impossible task until Tracy. If she had been killed by the same person who killed Stella, that could very well mean that the residents of Foxtail Lake had a vicious killer living among them.

Gracie was sitting at the kitchen table sipping a cup of coffee and reading the morning paper when I came downstairs this morning. Alastair followed me into the room and headed directly to his food bowl. I checked to make sure that Gracie had already filled it before pouring my own cup of coffee and joining her at the table.

"It seems that Alastair slept with me again. I hope you don't mind."

Gracie looked up. "Not at all, dear. There are times in all our lives when we need a kitty in our bed, and I think right now that you need him more than I do. Would you like some breakfast?"

"Just coffee for now." I took a sip of the hot brew. Gracie always had made the best coffee. She'd never shared her secret with me, but I thought she must add something to the grounds. Vanilla maybe?

"So, what are your plans today?" Gracie asked.

"I stayed around the house yesterday so I thought I'd go into town today. I need to run by the pharmacy to pick up some more of the cream the doctor has me using for my skin grafts, and I could use some shampoo and stuff. After that, I plan to head over the shelter to talk to Naomi about volunteering. Cass volunteers on Fridays, so I'll probably stay to work with him. We may go out for pizza afterward, so you probably shouldn't plan for me to be home for supper."

"It sounds like you have a full day."

"That's the plan. Sitting around and feeling sorry for myself isn't getting me anywhere."

Gracie stroked Alastair on the head. "I ran into Paisley when I was out checking on my garden after last night's rain. She mentioned that she'd asked you about piano lessons, but you told her you were busy."

"I didn't say 'busy.' I said, 'not staying long,'" I countered.

"Is that true? Are you not staying long?"

I blew out a breath. "Honestly, I'm not sure. I like Paisley. She seems like a nice kid, and lord knows she has a lot to deal with right now. It's just that I haven't touched a piano since the accident, and to tell you the truth, I'm not sure I'm ready to do it. Maybe I can do something else with her, and you can teach her to play the piano."

"That's fine. I understand." I could see that she didn't. "I'll talk to her. The poor dear really does need a friend, however, so if you have time to sit and chat with her, I think she'd enjoy that."

I nodded. "I'll make the time."

Gracie and I chatted for a while longer and then I went upstairs to shower and dress. It was odd to be back living in my childhood room. Don't get me wrong, it was a great room with its own bath and a large picture window that overlooked the lake. In addition to the bed and dresser, there was a seating area where a small divan and two armchairs framed a wood fireplace. Gracie had been talking about converting to gas for years because the fireplaces went a long way toward heating the house, but apparently, she hadn't gotten around to it.

I sat down at my makeup table and stared into the mirror. I hadn't figured out the next step in my life, but if I was going to stay for more than just a few weeks, I might want to think about making some changes. The pink-and-white-print wallpaper was dated, the linens on the bed almost two decades old, and even the white antique bookshelves looked out of date. My tastes had changed a lot since I'd lived in this room as a teen. Perhaps a room furnished in black and white, with black-and-white photos on the walls would be just the thing. Dark furniture, a light rug, and perhaps a patterned bedcover. The sofa was great, but the color was all wrong, so maybe I'd reupholster it in white and then do the armchairs in black. The bookshelves and dresser could be black as well, which would look nice against light walls. The more I thought about it, the more I liked the ideas. Of course, I'd need to talk to Gracie about them. This was, after all, her house.

The rain had returned by the time I drove into town. It was just sprinkling at this point, and the wind that had thundered through the area last evening had stilled to little more than a chilly breath. I doubted it would snow, but that was in our immediate future; I could feel it in my bones. Bones, I reminded myself, that were still healing from the pounding they'd taken in the accident. I still wasn't sure what had happened exactly. I'd gone over the event again and again in my mind, asking myself if I could have done anything better or differently to avoid what would end up being a career-ending event. I'd been on my way to rehearsal, humming to a tune that seemed to have planted itself in my head when, seemingly from out of nowhere, a car slammed into me. I'd never even seen it coming. The man driving the other car had not survived the accident. I wanted to feel bad about that, but as hard as I tried, I simply couldn't get there. They say that forgiveness is the key to moving on, but how was I supposed to forgive the person who'd decided it was a good idea to drink and drive only to end both our lives?

Once I reached the little downtown section of Foxtail Lake, I decided to park in the public lot and then walk up and down the street gathering the items I'd need. I'd brought my large shoulder tote to put everything in, and while the rain had steadied just a bit, I figured a little rain never hurt anyone. When I'd lived in New York, I'd actually walked quite a bit, preferring not to hassle with public transportation. I'd enjoyed the hustle and bustle of city life, but now that I was home in this tiny little town by the lake, I found the peace and quiet suited me as well.

"Callie Collins, is that really you?" asked Walter Bowman, the local pharmacist.

"It's really me," I replied.

"I heard you were back. It's so good to see you. It's been a while."

Pretty much everyone I'd run in to so far had made a similar comment, but I supposed they weren't wrong. "Too long," I agreed.

"So, how can I help you today?"

"I have a couple of prescriptions I need to have filled. I spoke to my doctor, and she said that if I got a phone number, she'd fax them over."

Walter handed me a form. "All the information you'll need to supply is right here. Are you staying long?"

"For a while. Long enough to need to transfer my prescriptions. Do you have any idea how long it will take to fill them once you receive the information from my doctor?"

"Depends on what you need. If you want to leave a phone number, I can call or text you when the prescriptions are ready."

I jotted down my cell number. "A text would be great." I looked around the tiny shop. "Does Jayme still work with you?"

Jayme, his daughter, worked the counter when I lived here before.

"She got married and moved to Aspen. She has two kids now and another one on the way."

I smiled. "That's great. I bet you love being a grandpa."

He bobbed his head. "I do at that. Even been thinking about selling this place and moving to Aspen so I can be close to her family. I'm the only one here in Foxtail Lake now, so it feels like it might be time to move on."

"I'll miss you if you go, but I totally understand. It seems like a lot of the folks who lived here when I was last in Foxtail Lake have moved away in the past fourteen years."

"Seems like it is getting harder and harder to make a living here. Besides, once young folks such as yourself move away, that only leaves us old geezers to carry on."

I supposed Walter had a point. It did seem that a larger-than-average percentage of the local population was qualified to receive a senior discount.

"The community board is near overflowing with homes for sale all of a sudden," he continued.

I glanced at the bulletin board, which was provided for locals to use to advertise community events, as well as items for sale. It did seem as if there were a lot of houses for sale. More than I remembered seeing in the past, not that I'd been old enough to pay all that much attention to such things when I lived here before.

I plucked one of the flyers off the wall. "It looks like they still need volunteers for the haunted barn."

"Last I heard, they were looking for volunteers for pretty much everything relating to this year's Harvest Festival. If you have time and are so inclined, you might want to talk to Hope Mansfield over at the library. She's the one who is organizing things this year. Or at least she was. I guess you heard about Tracy Porter."

I nodded. "It really is tragic."

"Hope was Tracy's godmother. It's understandable that she has been taking things hard. If I had to guess, the festival committee might have found someone to take over her duties so that she has the time she needs to grieve."

"I remember Hope from when I lived here before. I wasn't aware she was so close to Tracy. I should stop by to offer my condolences."

"Not sure if she is back to work yet. I know she took a few days off when Tracy's body was first found. Such a darn shame, the whole lot of it."

I thanked Walter and continued on my way. I hadn't planned to stop by the library, but if Hope, who I'd actually been friends with as a teen, had been close to the victim, I really did want to stop by to let her know how sorry I was. I remembered how hard it was for everyone when Stella died. It was like the light that shone down on the town went out completely during those first dark days of trying to deal with the reality of what someone had done.

The library was located at the end of a narrow lane off the main street that ran through town. As I climbed the somewhat steep hill leading to the small building as I had so many times before, I remembered the first time I'd been there. Hope was a young and eager woman who'd recently graduated college and started work at the library. Being full of the enthusiasm and energy of youth, she'd started a weekly book club. At the time, I was a high school freshman flunking English. When my teacher offered me a lifeline in the form of extra credit, I jumped at it. As it turned out, the extra credit I'd been offered consisted of joining and participating in Hope's book club for the rest of the semester. Not only had Hope and her book club helped me to get my grade up to a C, but Hope and the other members helped me to view reading as a pleasurable pastime and not simply the chore I'd always felt it to be.

"Is Hope in?" I asked the woman at the counter.

"She is, but she is working on quarterly reports today. Can I help you with something?"

"I'm actually just here to say hi and to inquire about volunteering for the Harvest Festival. Can you let her know that Callie Collins is here? And let her know if now isn't a good time, I can come back."

"Okay. Please wait here."

The woman disappeared down a short hallway, entering the office at the end. I looked around while I waited. The little library hadn't changed all that much in fourteen years. It looked like the walls might have been painted, and the carpet had been replaced with a wood floor, but otherwise, it looked much the same. Hope had been a decade older than me when we'd met, but we seemed to have a lot in common and had become fairly good friends before I left.

"Callie Collins." Hope held her arms out to me. I stepped into them and accepted her hug. "How have you been?"

"Actually, I've been better," I admitted.

She offered me a look of sympathy. "I heard about your accident. I'm sorry. Why don't you come back to my office and we can chat?"

"I'd like that." I followed her down the short hallway. She indicated that I should take a seat across the desk from where she sat, and I did.

"I'm glad you stopped by," she said. "I've been meaning to stop by your aunt's house to say hi, but…"

"I heard about Tracy. I understand that she was your goddaughter."

Hope nodded. "Her mother and I were college roommates. Beth came to Foxtail Lake to visit me right around the time you graduated high school and left town. She met Steve, Tracy's father, and stayed." She dabbed at the moisture in the corner of her eye. "I just don't understand how this could have happened. Tracy was such a sweet girl. Why would anyone want to hurt her?"

"Do you remember Stella Steinmetz?" I asked

Hope nodded. "Sure. She was that girl who was found murdered while I was away at college. I'm afraid I don't remember the specifics; I was busy with my own life then, but I seem to remember you saying during one of our book club discussions that the murdered girl had been your friend."

"Best friend. And the reason I bring it up now is because Tracy's death and Stella's are very similar."

"How so?"

I explained the similarities, including the claw marks.

"That is odd." Hope was frowning by this point. I could tell that she was considering the ramifications of what I'd told her. "Do you think the same person who killed Stella killed Tracy?" she finally asked.

I nodded. "I think that might be the case. The fact that the murders occurred twenty years apart would make it seem that the cases couldn't be connected, but I found a third victim, another twelve-year-old girl on her way home from school, who was found in a shallow grave ten years ago. She didn't live in Foxtail Lake, but she did live in a town nearby, and her remains also revealed evidence of claw marks."

Hope leaned forward, resting her forearms on the desk in front of her. She steepled her fingers, tapping them lightly against one another. "So if the same person killed all three girls, how do we prove it? An even better question, how do we figure out who it was?"

"I don't know. Yet. I've been looking into it, and of course, Cass has been working on it. It seems to me that if we can figure out why the specific victims were chosen, we might be able to figure out who would have wanted to kill them."

"Makes sense."

"I know quite a bit about Stella. Her habits, her hobbies, her friend and family connections. We were, after all, best friends. I'm here because I hoped you could tell me about Tracy. Maybe if we can find commonalities between the two, we can find a link to the third girl."

Hope opened her desk drawer and took out a yellow legal pad. "Is it okay if I take notes while we chat?"

I shrugged. "Fine with me."

Hope wrote down Tracy's name, and then she sat for a minute drumming her pen on the pad beneath her hand. I waited, figuring she was searching for a place to start.

"Tracy was a friendly and popular girl. She did well in school, had a lot of friends, and participated in several after-school activities, including soccer and dance. She had two half brothers who were much older and never lived with her. She seemed to get along with her parents as well as a twelve-year-old girl can." Hope paused. "She was artistic. She even had some drawings in a local art show. She was funny, and she smiled a lot. Her eyes sparkled when she laughed. God, I miss her."

I leaned forward and placed a hand over Hope's. "I know. I'm sorry. I know it is hard to talk about this. To be honest, I'm not sure that talking about the girls will help, but I feel like I need to do something, and it's the only thing I can think of."

Hope took a tissue from her drawer and wiped her eyes. "It's fine. I agree that if we can find a significant link, that could help us narrow in on the killer." She looked down at her pad. She wrote the words *middle school*. "Both Stella and Tracy went to the same middle school. Maybe the killer works there."

"I had the same thought, though Hillary was killed walking home from a school thirty miles from here."

Hope rolled her eyes, tapping her pen on her pad. "Okay, what about a substitute teacher? A sub might work for both our middle school and the one in the next town."

My eyes widened. "That's good. I hadn't thought of that. A substitute teacher who has been around for twenty years might be a good lead to follow."

"Or a support person who might work as a temp for, say, the office or cafeteria."

"Also good leads." I leaned back just a bit. "I wonder how we can get a list of people who might meet that criterion."

"I guess we tell Cass what we figured out and ask him to get the records. Once we have them, I'd be willing to look at them to see if anyone stands out as having a particular link to Tracy."

"That would be great." I scooted forward in my chair. "I'll call you after I talk to Cass. He will want to speak to you as well."

"I'll be here or at home." Hope jotted down a phone number. "This is for my cell. You can call me at this number at any time. Let's find this lowlife and make him pay for what he did."

"I'm with you all the way." I stood up. "By the way, I almost forgot. I seem to have quite a bit of free time on my hands, so I thought I'd volunteer for the annual Harvest Festival. I understand that you are the person to see about that."

"I am, and I can use all the volunteers I can round up. There is a meeting tomorrow at ten right here in the library for everyone who has offered to help out. We're on a tight schedule, so by the end of the meeting, I'm hoping that everyone will have their assigned duties. Can you attend?"

"I'll be here." I looked at my watch. "Right now, I need to get over to the shelter. I have an appointment with Naomi to talk about a volunteer gig with her as well. But I'll be here in the morning, ready to do whatever needs to be done."

"Now that's what I like to hear. I'll see you then."

CHAPTER 8

Naomi and I might have been close in high school, but she tended to be a friendly extrovert who spent a lot of her time involved in both school and community activities, and I was something of a loner who, other than hanging out with Cass, spent most of my time daydreaming in the attic or practicing the piano. Not that I didn't have friends, but other than Stella and Cass, I can't say that I really had many close friends. Naomi was nice enough, and I enjoyed spending time with her during our volunteer hours, but I supposed in my heart I knew I was leaving this sleepy, small town as soon as I was able, so why put a lot of time into cultivating intimate relationships there? I'm sure there were those who would say that I was afraid of bonding with anyone after I lost Stella, and perhaps they'd be right.

Naomi was sitting on her front porch bottle feeding a tiny puppy when I arrived at the shelter. There were three other teeny, tiny puppies in the box next to the rocker. I bent down to take a look while she hummed a soft tune and gently rocked the newborn in her arms.

"They're so tiny," I said, sliding into the rocker next to her.

"Born yesterday," she replied.

"And the mama dog?"

"I'm afraid she didn't make it."

"Can I help?"

She nodded. She handed me the pup she'd been feeding and the bottle he'd been eating from, then made another bottle for the next pup in line. It took a lot of dedication to do what she did. These pups would probably need to be fed around the clock for quite some time. I wondered if she took on such a huge task on her own or if she had volunteers who took one or more of the pup's home.

"How often do they need to eat?" I asked.

"Every four hours in the beginning."

I smiled down at the tiny baby in my arms. "That seems like a big commitment."

"It is, but I'll happily do it if need be." She began to rock back and forth with the next pup in line. "I may not have to, however."

"And why is that?" I began rocking the pup in my arms the way I'd seen Naomi do it.

"I have a surrogate on the way. If the pups and the surrogate bond, I'll send the pups home with the woman who offered the service of her dog."

I frowned. "Surrogate?"

Naomi adjusted the pup in her arms. "My friend, Kimmy, has a golden retriever who is in the process of weaning her own pups. They do well drinking regular puppy formula mixed with kibble from a bowl, so Kimmy had the idea of trying to wean them early and introducing these pups to her mama dog in the hope that she'd nurse them. I've tried something similar in the past. Sometimes it works, and sometimes it doesn't. The key to the whole thing is using a surrogate who is laid back enough to accept the new pups as her own. Luckily, Beatrice is about as laid back as they come."

"Beatrice is Kimmy's mama dog?"

Naomi nodded.

I smiled at the pup in my arms. "I hope it works out. It does seem like it would be the best solution for these little guys. I'm sure they will be fine either way, but it seems as if little ones need the love and nurturing of a mother, or at least a mother substitute."

"I agree. It would be the best solution. If it doesn't work out, I'll be in for a few weeks of long nights. It isn't fun, but I've done it before, and I'm sure I'll do it again."

I finished feeding the pup in my arms and went on to the next one. "One of the reasons I came early was to talk to you about volunteering. I enjoy working with Cass and plan to continue to come by on Tuesday and Friday afternoons, but I have time on my hands right now and would like to do more."

"I can always use help. Do you know anything about dog training?"

"Not a thing," I answered honestly.

"I can show you what to do. As I explained before, I like to put all my dogs through a basic training class before I put them up for adoption. I need volunteers to work with the dogs going through the current class. It is best if they can practice the behaviors they are learning every day."

"That seems like a big commitment."

"It is, but the key to success is constant reinforcement of the behavior. If you're interested, I can train you on what to do, and once you feel confident, I can assign you one or more two-hour shifts a week."

"The dogs train for two hours?"

"Thirty minutes each, which includes ten minutes of play, so each volunteer can do four dogs in the two hours. I have ten dogs in the class right now. They really need to be worked six days a week at a minimum, so that is sixty sessions, which equates to fifteen volunteer shifts. So far, I have twelve of those shifts covered and am looking for volunteers to take on the other three."

"So I would commit to a two-hour shift where I would show up and work with four dogs for thirty minutes each to reinforce the training they receive in your class?" I clarified.

"Exactly. Are you interested?"

"I am. When do you need me?"

"The three shifts I have open are on Tuesdays, Thursdays, and Fridays. The time of day doesn't matter, so I allow my volunteers to set their own schedules. You plan to be here to work with Cass on Tuesday and Friday afternoons, so I sort of hoped you'd come early on those two days and knock out two of the three open shifts."

I nodded. "Okay. I'm in. I've never trained a dog in my life, but I'm willing to learn."

"That's all I ask. I have a training class on Monday. Would you be willing to come to observe? That will give you an overview of what we do. If you think you can make it work, we'll start working you and one of the dogs on Tuesday."

I glanced down at the tiny pup in my arms. I wondered what would happen to him. I wondered how his life would end up. I wondered if he'd find a forever home where he was loved and treated like one of the family, or if he'd end up abandoned and alone. I hoped that if the latter were true, he'd end up here with Naomi. "Okay. I'll be here on Monday. What time?"

"Four. I'll introduce you to my other trainers. They can help you if you find you need help and I'm not around."

How on earth had Callie Collins ended up with a gig as a dog trainer? I'd never even owned a dog. But as Naomi had said, the dogs and I could train and learn together.

"Looks like Cass is here," she said, nodding at the road leading to the kennel as an SUV approached.

"Do you need help with the last pup?" I asked.

"I'll feed him. The two of you can take a group of dogs out for a run around the property. A well-exercised dog is a happy dog, and happy dogs tend to find the best homes."

Once Cass got out of the vehicle, we all chatted for a few minutes, and then Cass and I headed to the kennel to pick up the dogs we would walk. The entire fifty acres was fenced, and there was a trail circling the perimeter, so we walked within the fencing with a larger group then we'd be able to handle if we ventured off the property. It had continued to rain off and on, so the trail was muddy, but I'd worn old work boots I'd left at Gracie's when I left the lake house, so I figured I'd be fine. Cass knew which dogs would walk politely off leash and which needed to be on a leash at all times, so he chose eight dogs from the first group, and we headed out.

"It looked like you've already been promoted to nursery duty," Cass commented as we walked.

"Naomi just happened to be feeding the pups when I arrived to talk to her about volunteering, so I pitched in. She said she has a surrogate she hopes will nurse the pups coming by later this afternoon. I hope it works out."

"Me too. It would be best for the pups." Cass paused to call one of the dogs who'd gotten too far ahead back to our side. I was going to need to learn everyone's name if I was ever going to do this on my own. I supposed that with time, I'd be able to identify each dog, but with the large turn over, I had no idea how Naomi and her volunteers kept track of everyone. "Did you get your volunteer hours worked out?"

"I did. I'm going to be here with you on Tuesdays and Fridays." I noticed that earned me a very sweet grin. "I'm also going to come early on both days and help out with the training program."

"Have you ever trained a dog before?"

"No, I haven't. In fact, I have very little experience being around dogs at all. But I'm a fast learner, and I want to help, so Naomi said she'd train me to train the dogs. I'm going to come on Monday to observe the beginner's class."

Cass took my hand in his as we neared the little pond Naomi had added to the property. It was cool bordering on cold today, so the dogs didn't seem interested in swimming, but I was willing to bet that during the summer they all would have waded in.

"The key to dog training is confidence and patience. Make sure whichever dog you are working with knows you are boss and that you will stand there all day until you get the behavior you are after, so he or she may as well give in and do what you ask so that you can both move on. It took me a while to get the hang of it, but now I've graduated to helping with the S and R training."

"S and R? You mean search and rescue?"

Cass nodded. "Naomi has a team, of which Milo and I are members. We can't always go on rescues with the others because most of the time when someone is missing Milo and I are on-duty for the sheriff's department. But we train with the team and participate in rescues when we can. Once you are comfortable with the ins and outs of dog training, I'm sure Naomi would be happy to work with you in this advanced capacity if you are interested and if you were staying in Foxtail Lake."

"I understand that being a member of the team would be a huge commitment, and she wouldn't want to spend time training anyone with one foot out the door."

"Exactly."

"Honestly, I have no idea what my long-term plans are, so I think I'll stick to basic training for now." One of the dogs, a husky I was pretty sure Cass had called Thor, trotted over with a stick. I accepted it from him and then gave it a toss. "I spoke to Hope over at the library today," I said after the dog took off running. "Did you know she was Tracy's godmother?"

"I did."

Of course, he did. He was a deputy. "Anyway, we got to talking about her death and how it seemed to mirror Stella's. We discussed the fact that a good candidate for a suspect would be someone who worked at the middle school because that was where both girls were seen last, but then I told her about Hillary, the girl I called to tell you about, who disappeared from Rivers Bend ten years ago. After we chatted a bit, we decided it might be a good idea to look at those men and women who temped for the county and worked out of all the schools in the area. The time span has been twenty years, so we figured there wouldn't be many if any subs who met those criteria."

"There are three."

"So you already thought to look?"

He nodded. "I've also interviewed the three. Veronica Jones has been a substitute teacher for thirty years and has taught at every school in the county."

"Thirty years. That's a long time. I wonder why she didn't apply for a full-time position."

"I asked her about that when we spoke, and she told me that she enjoyed the flexibility and variety that came with subbing. She didn't want to get bogged down teaching a single grade or subject in any one school."

"I guess that makes sense. Was she teaching at our middle school when Stella and Tracy disappeared and in Rivers Bend when Hillary disappeared?"

"She told me she didn't remember where she was working ten and twenty years ago, so I'm having her employment records pulled. She did say that she had been subbing for the history teacher on the day Tracy went missing. The woman was nice enough and didn't seem the sort to be a serial killer, but I'll keep her on my suspect list until I can confirm her whereabouts on the days Stella and Hillary disappeared."

When the dog with the stick returned, I accepted it and tossed it again. "Okay, who else do you have who fits the criteria?"

"Harvey Underwood, also a substitute teacher. He was new to the district when Stella went missing. He didn't remember which school he was working at or if he was even working on the day Stella went missing, but he did say that by the time Hillary went missing he'd landed a full-time teaching job in Rivers Bend. He remembered Hillary and the panic everyone felt when she turned up missing. He also said he remembered the horror that replaced the panic when Hillary's body was found."

"If he had a full-time teaching job in another town, he wouldn't have been here when Tracy went missing," I pointed out.

"Actually, he was. About four years ago, the county underwent budget cuts, and the arts and music programs were cut. Harvey had been teaching art and shop classes in Rivers Bend, so he found himself unemployed. He went back to subbing and admitted to having been here in Foxtail Lake subbing for a middle-school math teacher on the day Tracy disappeared."

"Seems like quite the coincidence."

"I agree. I'm not ready to state unequivocally that Harvey Underwood is the guy we are looking for, but I did pick up an odd vibe from him. He appeared to be cooperating, and he did answer every question I asked, but the entire time we were talking, I had this feeling there was something he wasn't saying."

"So are you going to dig into his past?"

"I am. I'm waiting for verification as to where he was teaching on the day Stella went missing and then I'll take it from there."

"And the third suspect?" I asked, tossing the stick yet again.

"Ronald Trauner. He is a substitute custodian who works at all the schools in the county as he is needed. I hate to bring stereotypes into the conversation, but Mr. Trauner most definitely fits the description of the creepy custodian who never really interacts with anyone but watches everyone and everything and knows exactly what is going on at all times."

"So he could totally have done it."

"When I first met him, I was sure he had. I remembered the guy from when we were in school. To be honest, he sort of freaked me out then and he most definitely still freaks me out now. I even felt a moment of fear despite the fact that I had a gun and all he had was a mop."

I frowned. "Do you mean that really tall guy with the black eyes and pale, pale complexion?"

Cass nodded.

"I totally remember him. He looked like a zombie. He was so pale, had sunken cheeks and dark eyes and never spoke. Even if you asked him a question, he sort of replied with a grunt. I figured he was mute."

"He can speak," Cass assured me. "He has a deep voice and he speaks slowly, as if considering each word before he says it. He answered my questions, but he was extremely monosyllabic. His answers consisted of one or two words for most of the interview."

"Was he at the right schools on the right days?"

"I don't know. I'm waiting for his employment records as well."

"You'd think the staff at the county would be all over getting the records to you, given the situation."

"You would think, but apparently, what seems urgent to us isn't urgent to them. I have a lot of data to go through this weekend. I have a list of suspects, but if you are correct in your opinion that Hillary was killed by the same person who killed both Stella and Tracy, that changes things quite a bit."

"Is the sheriff still bent on pinning Tracy's death on the homeless man from the campground?"

"He is. I have the feeling the guy might end up pleading guilty and trying for a lesser sentence. At this point, he has pleaded no contest and is working with his attorney on a strategy. I'm not sure what their end game is, but it is beginning to appear to me that there is a strategy in the man's unwillingness to offer a real defense."

I tossed the stick a final time as we approached our starting point. "It seems as if we are missing something. Something big. So far, if you take all the facts into account, nothing makes sense."

CHAPTER 9

Saturday

Gracie and I arrived at the library to find the reading room packed with men and women anxious to find out their assigned Harvest Festival duties. As a child and a teen, I'd attended the festival as a visitor, but I'd never stopped to consider the hundreds of man-hours that went into making the event happen. Hope started off by thanking everyone and reminding them that the festival was an important fund-raiser for the town as well as an important income-producing weekend for the small businesses that lined the main drag where the event was held. She briefly went over all the various volunteer duties, including the haunted barn, food vendors, kiddie carnival volunteers, and the pumpkin patch, among others. She sent around a clipboard with dates and times and asked everyone to sign up for whichever duties they were interested in. There was also a column for those of us who were flexible and willing to be used where needed. That is the column where I signed my name. My schedule was a lot more flexible than that of most of the men and women in the room, so I figured I'd be flexible too. There was a space to indicate times I was not available, and I entered Monday morning from ten to twelve, when I'd be at Naomi's training class, and Tuesday and Friday afternoon between two and six, when I would also be at the shelter. By the time the assignments were handed out, I ended up with a spot on the decorating committee tomorrow in the late morning and an early afternoon at the barn that would be used as a haunted house, a three-hour shift selling tickets at the barn on Friday night from seven to ten, and a four-hour shift manning a booth at the kiddie carnival on Saturday morning from ten to two. Suddenly, I felt like I had a full week. Being busy, I realized, was a state of being I was very much ready for.

Once Gracie and I had received our assignments and we'd both made small talk with a group of people we knew, we headed back to the lake house. Gracie planned to use the afternoon to finish winterizing her garden with Tom's help, and I'd decided to clean and organize the attic with Alastair's help. The room under the rafters really was the place I felt the most comfortable. It was still where I most wanted to spend time every day. I supposed this deep-seated appreciation for the space had been rooted in childhood, but I was happy to say that the feeling of peace and contentment I found while sitting in the window seat overlooking the lake was the same feeling of peace and contentment I'd found as a child.

"I wonder why Gracie has all this glassware up here," I said to Alastair, who was sitting in the window watching me struggle to lift and move boxes with my injured hand. "It seems if the glassware is functional, she'd have it in the kitchen, and if she no longer was interested in using it, she'd donate it to the women's auxiliary at the church."

"Meow."

I shoved the box aside. "Yeah. I guess I should ask her." I glanced out the window. Gracie was working just below it, so I opened it and leaned out. "I've come across several boxes of glasses. Is there a particular reason you're saving them?" I called down.

"Blue glasses of various sizes?" she called back up.

"That would be them."

"The kitchen used to be blue, but when I redecorated, the blue glasses and dishes no longer matched. I just stuck everything up in the attic."

"Maybe we can donate them to the women's auxiliary at the church."

"That's a good idea," Gracie said.

"Do they still hold a rummage sale once a month?"

"They do. They use the money for little extras, like flowers. Just push the boxes aside, and I'll help you carry them down later. I can drop everything off tomorrow after services."

I pushed the boxes out into the little hallway and continued to open and close boxes, which I then either pushed into the hallway for donation or stacked against a wall to keep.

"What are you doing?"

I turned around and found Paisley standing in the doorway.

"Paisley! I didn't hear you come up the stairs." I glanced around the cluttered room. "I'm cleaning the attic, so I have more room to move around."

"Can I help?"

I noticed the hope in the young girl's eyes. "Sure. As long as you have on something you won't mind getting dirty. It's pretty dusty up here."

She grinned. "I don't mind the dust. What should I do?"

Good question. I looked around the room until I noticed a box I knew was filled with old clothing. "We are going to donate a lot of this stuff to the church auxiliary. These three boxes are full of old clothes. If you want to help, you can go through the boxes and try to pare things down a bit. Maybe we can donate two boxes of clothes and keep one."

Paisley crossed the room. She opened the box. "What sort of things are you looking to keep?"

"Anything that is particularly interesting. When I was a kid, I used to play dress-up with the clothes in those boxes. Many of my Halloween costumes came from there as well. If you find anything like a formal dress a princess might wear or a leather vest befitting a pirate, keep it. If it is an old T-shirt or boring wool slacks, toss it. If you aren't sure, ask me."

"Okay."

I returned to my work on the other side of the room while Paisley began sorting the clothes. She'd started by making two piles, one to donate and one to keep. That was a good idea because it afforded her the opportunity to take a second look at everything as she put the piles back into the boxes. While she did that, I started moving the furniture I knew Gracie would want to keep toward the back of the room.

"I love this." Paisley stood up. She held an old gown with a full skirt that had belonged to some long-ago ancestor in front of her.

"I used to wear that dress all the time when I was your age. Whichever Hollister it belonged to must have been petite because it wasn't all that long on me. Either that or someone hemmed it at some point."

Paisley twirled around. "It seems like something someone would wear to a ball. Someone like Cinderella."

"I used to play Cinderella when I was a kid. I'd make Archie wear a vest Gracie had made for him, and he would be both my fairy godfather and my coachman."

"Archie?"

"The family cat at the time." I glanced at Alastair. He was still watching us, but he hadn't moved from his place in the window.

"What about a prince?"

I smiled. "I had a friend named Cass, and sometimes I would give him some of my best trading cards to be my prince. Other times I'd dress up the dressmaker's mannequin and twirl it around the room." I glanced around the room. "There used to be a large hanging chair up here that I would use as my magical carriage."

"Do you still have it?"

I bit my lower lip. "I'm not sure. I guess we can look for it. It was this egg-shaped thing that hung from the top. You could slip in through one side and sit on the cushion." I didn't see anything that stood out as being egg-shaped, but there was a lot of stuff stacked in the attic, and most of it was covered. I headed toward the back of the room. I didn't find the chair, but I did find a box of old photo albums. I picked the first one from the top.

"Who's that?" Paisley had come up behind me, and now she pointed to a photo of my parents. "The lady looks just like you."

"That's my mother, and the handsome devil next to her is my father."

"They don't live here anymore?"

I slowly moved my head from left to right. "No. They don't live here. They were killed in a car accident when I was four years old. Aunt Gracie raised me, which is why I grew up here."

I slipped down onto the floor, crossing my legs in front of me. I slowly turned the pages of the old album, desperately trying to remember people I simply couldn't. Sure, I was able to pull up small frames of memory, but the pictures in my mind were totally devoid of emotion.

"How was it being raised by someone who was not your mother?" Paisley asked after a while.

That seemed like a mature question to be coming from a ten-year-old.

"I don't remember a lot of things from that time. I was only four, but I do remember being sad and scared. But then Aunt Gracie brought me up here and showed me all the magical things she had stored. I spent a lot of time up here pretending, and then, as time went by, things got better. I remember my childhood as being a happy one if that is what you are asking."

Paisley sat down next to me. She leaned her head against my shoulder. "My grandma is going to raise me when my mom dies."

I turned slightly to give the child my full attention. "I know you said your mom was sick. I didn't realize she was dying. I'm so sorry."

"Everyone is trying to protect me. They keep saying that the doctor is waiting on a miracle to help him know what to do to make Mom better. At first, I wasn't worried, but then I heard Mom and Grandma talking. They didn't know I was listening. Mom was telling Grandma that there was nothing more the doctors could do. She was telling her that it would be up to her to take care of me when she was gone. Grandma kept trying to tell her not to give up. She said they just needed a miracle and everything would be fine. I don't think Mom believed her, though. She was crying like her heart was breaking."

Oh, God. Now *my* heart was breaking. I fought the tightness in my chest. I knew that what I said at this point was probably going to be important, but I had no idea what it was going to be. I decided I had to speak from my heart. "I don't know what is going to happen with your mother, but I do agree with your grandmother that sometimes when all hope seems gone, depending on a miracle is really all you can do." I looked down at my hand. "During those first awful days and weeks after my car accident, the doctors told me I would never again have use of this hand. They said that all the nerves had been severed and I would never even be able to use my fingers." I held up my hand and wiggled my fingers. "But see, they were wrong. Everyone said that it is a miracle that I have any use of my hand at all. My doctor said there is no medical explanation for the fact that my ability to use my fingers and manipulate my hand is slowly returning. Do you know what you have when something that is impossible happens?"

"A miracle?"

"Exactly. I don't know why some people get miracles, and some don't. To be honest, I've always struggled with the big questions. But I do know that if you define a miracle as the existence of something that should not have happened but did, then from my own experience, I know they are possible."

Paisley wiped a stray tear from her cheek. "So even if the doctor thinks there is no hope, that doesn't mean that a miracle can't happen?"

"Exactly. And even if it doesn't, even if your mom's time here on this earth is up, I also know it is possible to find happiness despite the circumstance. I was happy here with Aunt Gracie, and I bet you can be happy with your grandmother. I've never met her, but I have a feeling she is nice. Very nice."

Paisley nodded. "She is. And she smells good too. Like vanilla." Paisley looked down at my hand. She ran a finger over my scar. "Does it hurt?"

"Not really. Sometimes it gets tingly, and that can be irritating, but the doctor said it is my nerves coming back to life. I might always have to deal with the tingly feeling, but if I can regain full use of the hand, it will be worth it."

"So you can go back to work?"

I slowly shook my head. "No. I'll never again be able to play the piano at that level. But it will be nice to be able to do other things like pick up a pin that has dropped to the floor."

"Can't you use your other hand to pick up a pin?"

"Well, sure. It's just that... Oh, never mind. Let's just say the more I can wiggle my fingers, the happier I'll be."

Paisley hugged me. "I'll pray for a miracle for you too."

I had to admit I was surprised by that. I hugged the girl back. "Thank you. I appreciate that, and I'll pray for a miracle for your mom." I slowly stood up. "In the meantime, I guess we should get back to this."

Over the next couple of hours, Paisley and I worked side by side. We chatted and laughed, and I shared memories that were ignited by the contents of almost every box we came across. It was good to revisit the time in my life when I supposed I'd been happiest. I didn't remember much of anything about the first four years of my life, and once I'd committed to a life as a concert pianist, happiness had been replaced with obsession, but for a while, as a child and a teen living here at the lake, I'd been happy. Really, really happy.

"Look at this," Paisley screeched, breaking me out of my daydream. "It's a piano." She pulled the sheet aside and tapped out a few keys.

I crossed the room. "This is the piano I first learned to play on. Eventually, Gracie bought the piano that is in her living room now, but it was on this old piano where I first fell in love with the melodies that surged through my soul."

"Can you play me something?"

I glanced down at my hand. "Oh no, I can't. Not anymore."

Paisley frowned. "Why not? Did you forget how?"

"No, I didn't forget how, but my fingers, while on the mend, don't work as well as they used to."

Paisley ran her hand along the keys. "Can you do that?"

"Well, sure."

"Will you?"

I took a deep breath. Would I? Well, that was a question I didn't want to answer.

"Please."

I pulled up the old bench and sat down. Paisley sat down beside me. I ran my fingers over the keys. "Happy?"

"Will you play a song? It can be an easy one. *Mary Had a Little Lamb*? That's the song everyone starts with."

"Okay, one song. One easy song." I played John Lennon's *Imagine.*

"Wow," Paisley said. "That was so good. Play another one."

"We agreed on one."

"I know. But it was so good. And you were smiling. You liked it too."

Did I? Was it even possible to find joy in music once again, given my limitations? *Imagine* was an easy song to play even with fingers that wouldn't always cooperate.

"Please," Paisley said.

"Okay. But I'm going to need your help."

Her eyes grew wide. "Really?"

"Really. Sit here on my left side."

She moved to the other side of the bench.

"I'm going to play the right side, and you play the left."

"But I don't know how to play the piano."

"This song is easy. Just four notes that repeat in the same pattern. Here, I'll show you."

Somewhere during that afternoon, while Paisley and I came up with a way to work together to create what I thought was some pretty great music, I found the fire I thought had died. When I was a child sitting at this piano, I'd played horribly, but I'd played from a place of love and connection. Somewhere along the way, that love and connection had been replaced by dedication and the search for perfection. I'd enjoyed my career while I'd had it, but when I'd shut out the imperfect melodies created by the music in my soul in favor of mechanical perfection, I'd lost the connection to my heart. Maybe, after all this time, it was waiting to be found once again.

CHAPTER 10

Sunday

I closed my eyes and cringed when I realized which barn we were heading toward. Of all the barns in all the world, why did the haunted barn have to be here? This barn and I had history, a very embarrassing history I'd just as soon forget.

"Something wrong, dear?" Aunt Gracie asked as she headed toward the dirt lot set up for parking.

"No. I just hadn't realized the haunted barn was going to be held here on old man Logan's property."

"The barn we used when you lived here before burned to the ground, and the town has been using this one for years. I seem to remember that you and Cass used to go fishing here at Logan Pond."

I tried to prevent the blush that I knew was about to redden my cheeks. "Yes. We did. When we were kids."

The truth of the matter was, in addition to fishing here as kids, Cass and I had shared our one and only kiss right here in this barn. Actually, it was more than a kiss, so very, very much more. It hadn't been planned and definitely hadn't been wise, but it had occurred nonetheless.

We'd been at the pond fishing, as we often did when it wasn't frozen over. The day had started out cool but had gotten hot, so we'd decided to go for a swim. We hadn't planned to swim, so we hadn't worn bathing suits, but we were kids, and Cass and I had swum together many times wearing just our underwear. I pulled off my T-shirt and shorts without giving it a second thought. As I stood before him in only my panties, while he wore only his boxers, I'd noticed a shift in his attention. It was early spring, and we hadn't swum together since the previous summer, so when I pulled off my shirt, I hadn't stopped to consider that I'd begun to develop breasts over the winter. I'm petite and small-breasted, and I was also a late bloomer, so the fact that I had breasts at all had sort of crept up on me. Long story short, our seemingly innocent swim had turned into something else altogether.

Not that anything had happened. Not really. We were, after all, just thirteen. But there was no denying the fact that the energy between us had changed on that muggy afternoon. An unforeseen storm had rolled in, and somehow we'd ended up in the old barn. I'm still not sure how it happened, but before that late spring storm had rolled through, we'd shared our first kiss.

I swallowed hard. My first kiss, if I was being perfectly honest. How naive had I been not to realize that a thirteen-year-old girl and a thirteen-year-old boy shouldn't swim together in only their underwear?

"Things have changed quite a bit since the last haunted barn you attended," Gracie continued, seemingly unaware that my heart was pounding and my face was flush. "Not only the location but things have become much more animated with all the new technology."

I glanced at the cars already parked in the lot, hoping that Cass's wouldn't be there, but as he'd indicated he would be, he was already here. The fact that I knew that he would remember the same thing I had had me blushing clear up to the roots of my hair.

"They have a mechanical skeleton that is actually quite lifelike. We've even had to post a warning for young children," Gracie continued. "It moves its arms and legs, and when the building is dark, and you can't see the cables, it looks like it is chasing you."

"Sounds like fun," I choked out.

"Personally, I worry that they've made it too frightening, though it is, after all, a haunted barn. I suppose children who are too young to attend still have a lot of child-friendlier options in town." Gracie pulled into a parking spot two cars down from where Cass had parked.

I took a deep breath and prayed that my face didn't look as hot and flustered as it felt.

Thankfully the place was packed with enthusiastic volunteers, and I was greeted immediately after walking through the door, which prevented the awkwardness of standing in front of the room looking for a friendly face. Gracie headed toward the back of the barn where a group from her bridge club were hanging rubber bats along the ceiling.

"Oh my God, Callie. I'm so happy you came."

"It's good to see you, Chelsea." I hugged the woman who was about to squeeze the life out of me. Not that I wasn't happy to see her. Chelsea Garber and I had been good friends back in the day.

"I heard about your accident. I just want you to know how sorry I am."

"Thank you." I smiled at the perky woman. "You look great. Very fit."

"I own a Pilates studio now. Can you believe that? I mean, I am the one who flunked out of PE when I was a sophomore because I didn't want to get sweaty, but then I found Pilates as an adult and fell in love with everything about it."

"Well, it seems to agree with you. As I said, you look fantastic."

"You should come by. It will totally change your life. Seriously, I can't say enough about not only the physical benefits but the mental and emotional ones as well."

"I'll keep it in mind." I looked around the barn. "I should probably check in with Hope. Have you seen her?"

"She's in the back under the loft. Just so you know, there have been a few hiccups and she has been somewhat frantic, so don't take it personally if she snaps at you."

I nodded. "Thanks for the warning. And it was nice to see you again."

"Don't forget to come by for a class. The first one is on the house."

"I will. And thanks." I put my head down and went toward the loft. While I was eager to catch up with everyone, having all the people I needed to catch up with all together in one place was overwhelming.

"Oh good, you made it." Hope smiled despite the fact that the smile seemed tense and almost forced.

"I'm here and ready to work. What do you want me to do?"

She held up two extension cords that were still rolled and wrapped in cardboard, indicating they were new. "Cass is up in the loft working on the electrical. Can you run these up to him?"

"Uh, sure," I replied, although I'd been hoping to delay our eventual meeting for a little while longer.

"Tell him that the long cord he wanted is on the way. They were out of them at the hardware store, so I sent someone to Rivers Bend to get one."

"Okay. I'm on it." I hoped my tone communicated confidence and not the nervousness I was feeling. I took a deep breath as I climbed the ladder to the loft. I was being ridiculous. I knew that. This was Cass. Arguably, the best friend I had left in the world, even though I'd gone more than a decade without seeing him. He knew all my dirty little secrets. No reason to be nervous. Right?

"Hey, Cass," I said as I stepped from the ladder onto the floor of the loft. "I have the extension cords you asked for. At least two of them. Someone had to drive to Rivers Bend to the get the extra-long one."

"Great. Just set them there on that bale of hay. Can you hand me those pliers?"

I did as requested. "The place really looks fantastic. Very high-tech compared to the haunted barns you and I attended as kids."

"Personally, I think the guy who designs this thing goes a little overboard with the mechanics, but I'm just here to help, so what do I know? Do you see a screwdriver around anywhere?"

I looked around the loft. "Yeah, hang on." Our hands touched as I handed him the tool he'd asked for, creating thoughts in my mind one should not have after just coming from church. "So, how did you end up being in charge of the electrical? Shouldn't they have an electrician see to such things?" I asked, trying to get my mind off the tingling in my fingers that might have been caused by the accident but might have been caused by something else altogether.

"Troy Wheeler from Wheeler Electrical came by and hooked up the electrical panel. I'm just figuring out which extension cords are going to run which gadgets."

"I remember Troy. Short with blond hair. He had an older brother. Tony."

"Yep. They both went to work for their father. Seems like they do okay." Cass stood up. He rubbed his lower back, I assumed to work out a kink. "Do you remember Vanessa Vanderbilt?"

"Sure, I remember Vanessa. She was a year behind us in school."

"She and Troy are married now, with three kids, a white picket fence, and a minivan. Did you ever think that Vanessa would be the sort to settle down and have a family?"

"Actually, no. She was, well, she was sort of …"

"Crazy," Cass supplied.

"Well, yeah. I was trying to come up with a kinder way to put it."

"If I had to guess, her teenage hormones got the best of her. She works for the middle school as a secretary, and as hard as it is to believe, she seems perfectly normal now."

I leaned a hip against the wall. "Middle school? Have you spoken to her about Tracy?"

He nodded. "When Tracy first went missing, I interviewed every single staff member. Of course, everyone was shocked about what had happened, and no one remembered seeing anything that would help me find her. I've spoken to a few of the staff since Tracy's body was found, but not Vanessa. I suppose I should call to set up an interview if the lead involving the three temp workers doesn't pan out."

"Do you think it will? Do any of the three seem like real suspects?"

"I didn't have the sense that Veronica Jones is the killer I'm looking for. When we spoke, she appeared to be a perfectly nice woman who really cares about the students she spends time with. As for Harvey Underwood, as I said on Friday, while nothing he said seemed to implicate him, I did get an odd vibe from him. If I had to guess, he is hiding something."

"And the creepy janitor?"

"If I had to pick one of the three as the killer, he'd be the one, but I've thought about it, and he didn't appear to know any of the three girls, and he really doesn't seem to have a motive, although I doubt motive was involved in any of the three deaths. Perhaps there is something ritualistic going on here."

"Okay, so what is the link? Why these three girls? Were they chosen, or were they in the wrong place at the wrong time?"

Cass groaned. "I wish I knew. Can you check to see if there is an electrical strip on that far wall?"

I crossed the musty loft and did as Cass asked. "Yeah, there is one of those safety strips tacked to the wall."

"Okay, great. I think we are in business."

He stood up and reached overhead to grab the end of an extension cord that had been fed up along one of the walls from somewhere downstairs. The movement exposed his belly just above his belt. The dark hair and firm abs left no doubt in my mind that Cass Wylander wasn't a kid any longer. He lowered his arms, and in that instant, he caught me staring. Nothing I could do could prevent the blush that followed. "I guess I should head downstairs to see what needs to get done."

"Thanks for your help."

I turned to leave and then turned back. "It's weird being here again."

He smiled. "I guess it is the first time we've been here together in this barn since that time we," he paused briefly, "went fishing in Logan Pond."

"Yeah." I couldn't help but remember Cass's hands on my body.

"Just so you know," Cass added as I turned toward the stairs once again, "I consider that to be the best fishing trip of my life."

I paused and looked him in the eye. "Yeah. Me too." With that, I climbed down the ladder.

CHAPTER 11

Monday

By the time the sun had begun its descent toward the horizon on the previous afternoon, the barn had been transformed into a house of horrors. The group that had shown up had consisted of both old friends and new neighbors I'd yet to meet. When I'd first returned to Foxtail Lake, I'd been broken both in body and spirit, but as I sat in the attic window watching it rain, it occurred to me that in the time I'd been here, both body and spirit had turned a corner and appeared well on the road to recovery.

"Is Alastair up there with you?" Aunt Gracie called up the stairs.

I smiled at the cat sitting beside me as I sipped my morning coffee. "Yes, he is up here."

"I need to run into town to do a few errands. Do you need anything?"

"No," I called back. "I'm going to finish my coffee, and then I am heading over to the shelter for my first dog training class. I'm not sure what time I'll be home."

"Okay, dear. Have fun."

"I will." I glanced out the window and wondered if Hope would even hold the class. Perhaps it was indoors. "It's raining pretty hard. Be careful. The roads will be slick, and I know your arthritis has been bothering you with all this funky weather."

"Tom is coming with me, so he'll drive."

I wasn't sure that was any better but all right.

I continued to watch out the window and saw Tom help Gracie into the car. He walked around to the driver's side, got in, and slowly drove away. Gracie had turned seventy on her last birthday, and I would guess that Tom was older than that. They were energetic and healthy for their age, and both appeared not to let the little aches and pains they did have slow them down. I glanced toward the lakeside cabin where Tom lived and wondered about his life before he'd been caretaker for Hollister House. I'd once heard Gracie say that he'd been here for more than forty years, but I had no idea what she'd meant exactly by *more than*. If he was, say, seventy-five, *more than* could mean he'd first started working here when he was thirty-four. It could also mean that he'd been working and living on the land since his twenties. Maybe one day I'd ask Gracie exactly how it was that he had come to live here.

I glanced out at the lake. Heavy clouds hung over the surface, cloaking the shoreline that extended beyond the Hollister property line. When it was dark and overcast like this, and the wind pushed the water toward the shore, Foxtail Lake looked more like an ocean than a lake. I loved the lake in all its moods. I loved it when it was dark and brooding, as it was today, and I loved it when it was a deep royal blue that contrasted the white dots on the surface created by a dusting of sailboats and geese.

Sliding my feet to the floor, I stood up and looked around the attic. Paisley and I had done a stellar job getting the place cleaned up on Saturday. The boxes and furnishings we'd decided to keep were neatly labeled and stacked, leaving room to move around. I crossed the room and sat down at the old piano. I'd been so sure I'd never play again, and I wouldn't, at least not with the same perfection I once had, but somewhere along the way, I'd forgotten that an imperfect melody from the heart meant much more than a precise and accurate stroke of the keys. I slowly moved my fingers over them, pecking out a simple song. I let the joy I'd felt as a child playing this very song penetrate my shattered heart. I could spend the rest of my life mourning what could and should have been, or I could pick up the pieces of my life and move on.

On any other rainy day, with the house empty and Alastair as my only critic, I might have tested the limits of my new condition, but today I had a dog training class to get to, so I closed the piano lid,

called to the cat, and headed downstairs to shower
and dress.

CHAPTER 12

When I arrived at the shelter, the parking area was fairly full. Naomi had texted to let me know that the training class was going to be held in the indoor area where Cass and I'd played with the dogs that first day because the rain hadn't let up and the forecast didn't call for it clearing anytime soon. The dirt lot was muddy, making me wish I'd worn my old boots rather than my new tennis shoes. Oh, well a little dirt never hurt anyone.

"Callie, I'm so glad you made it," Naomi greeted me as I walked into the room.

"I'm eager and ready to learn."

"That's really great. All I really want you to do today is sit and watch. Watch the trainers, watch the dogs, and listen to my instructions. Maybe visualize what you would do and how you would handle specific situations should they arise. If you are free, I thought maybe you could stay after. I'll make us some lunch, and we can talk about what happened, what to expect, and some of the scenarios you might be faced with when you are assigned a dog of your own."

I nodded. "That sounds great, and yes, I can stay. I have nowhere to be until three when Paisley is due to come by for her first official piano lesson."

Naomi smiled. "You know Paisley?"

"She lives near Gracie and comes around sometimes to hang out with her. I just met her a few days ago, but I think we've really bonded."

"That's fantastic. She really needs someone." She looked toward the group that was still gathering. "I need to get started, but we'll talk more later."

The class I observed seemed simple enough. Each human had been assigned a dog that they put through the paces Naomi described. She had them practice sit, down, stay, come, and heel. After every few minutes of training, the dogs would be given a minute or two of snuggle time with their trainer. The group must have been training together for a while because everyone seemed to know what to do even before Naomi demonstrated the desired behavior. I did notice that some dogs seemed to understand what they needed to do right away and others seemed preoccupied and needed to be given the command several times, but in the end, Naomi had everyone doing what they were supposed to be doing.

After the class ended, Naomi introduced me to the other trainers and explained that I would be taking on a couple practice sessions. I guess there were some trainers who took the dogs through their paces in the class with other dogs, and other trainers who came during the week and practiced the commands learned in the class with the dogs individually. That was where I came in. I had zero experience with dogs, so I really, really hoped I'd be up to the task.

Once everyone had left, we headed to Naomi's house. It was a nice home, simple yet cozy. The wooden structure had log walls, a wood floor, and big windows that overlooked a gorgeous meadow and a seasonal stream.

"Have a seat at the table," Naomi instructed.

I sat down at the round table that was tucked into a nook. There was a vase with wildflowers on the table that I pushed to the side to make more room. "Your home is lovely."

"Thanks. It's small, but I love it."

"The rock fireplace is great. I bet it is very cozy in here on a snowy winter day."

"It is. The cabin is cozy anyway, given its tiny size, but when you add the crackle of a wood fire and a gentle snow, it's magical."

I looked around the room, which contained a small kitchen, good-sized living area, and a small dining nook. It appeared there was a bathroom tucked under the stairs, but I didn't see any other rooms. "I take it you sleep up in the loft?"

Naomi nodded. "There is a pretty large space up there. I not only sleep in it, but I have a desk in a small office area upstairs as well. Are you okay with onions?"

"Sure. I liked onions."

Naomi set two sandwiches on the table. There were tons of yummy veggies in them, layered onto thick slices of whole grain bread. "I hope veggie is okay. After working with the animals for a while, I went vegetarian," she explained.

"Veggie is great. Do you eat eggs? Cheese?"

"I have a neighbor who gives me milk and eggs, which I know have been provided by animals who are treated as members of the family, and I will sometimes eat cheese, but generally speaking, any animal product I consume needs to come from a source I am familiar with. I suppose my biggest exception is when Hancock is here. He loves pizza and will agree to veggie, but he refuses to skimp on the cheese."

"Hancock?"

"My neighbor and sort of boyfriend. Actually, he is not so much a boyfriend as a lover."

"I see. Is Hancock his first name or last?"

Naomi shrugged. "I have no idea. When we met, he told me to call him Hancock. I don't know if Hancock is his first name, last, or neither, but in the end, I suppose it doesn't matter. Everyone calls him Hancock, so if you mention the name to anyone in town, people will know who you are talking about."

I supposed if it worked for them, it worked for me. "I look forward to meeting him."

"Hancock is in naval intelligence. He is away as often as he is here, and you never know when he might pop in or out or how long he will be gone when he is away."

"That must be difficult."

Naomi shrugged. "Not for me. Like I said, ours is a friendship with benefits. I enjoy him when he is here, but I do fine when he is away as well. To be honest, if he was around twenty-four/seven, I'd probably want to shoot him. He is very sweet and very good-looking, but he is very intense."

"I guess working in naval intelligence would require him to be somewhat intense." I glanced around the room, enjoying the feeling of comfort Naomi had created. "I take it he is away now?"

She nodded. "He is. Been away almost two weeks. I have no idea where he is or when he'll be back, but I'll welcome him with open arms when he does show up. I have a fruit cobbler for dessert if you'd like some."

"That sounds great." I got up and took my plate to the dishwasher. "Do any of the dogs live here in the house with you?"

"Just Humper. He's an old hound dog that is blind in one eye." She glanced around the room. "I built a ramp so he could get up into the loft, so I'm betting he is up there taking a nap. He takes a lot of naps."

"Why do you call him Humper?"

She raised a brow.

"Oh. I see."

"He isn't as bad as he was when he was younger, but it is best to let him know right off the bat where your boundaries lie."

"I'll remember that." I followed Naomi out of the kitchen as she set the bowls of cobbler on the table and offered me coffee, which I accepted. It was nice sitting here in this charming little cabin having lunch with someone I knew from high school while the rain pitter-pattered on the roof. I never had any girlfriends after Stella. In fact, after Stella died, it was really just Cass and me. I mean, we had a circle of people we hung out with from time to time, but I never really bonded or shared my secrets with anyone other than Cass once Stella was no longer in my life.

"So tell me about your life after you left here," Naomi said after setting a cup of hot coffee and a carton of almond milk in front of me.

"There isn't a lot to tell. I pursued a career as a concert pianist, traveled the world a bit, was T-boned by a drunk driver, and ended up right back here."

"Any serious relationships?"

"Not a one." I took a sip of the coffee. "How about you? Anyone who was more than a friend with benefits?"

"I lived with a wonderful man named Jordan for two years. I really loved him. Might even have married him despite my negative views on that subject, but he died in a climbing accident five years ago."

"I'm so sorry."

"Yeah. Me too. He was a pure and genuine soul. In some ways, I feel like a part of me died with him, but I have my cozy home and my animals. I do okay."

I supposed I wasn't the only one who had lost the thing closest to my heart only to be left with a broken life to see me into the future. The conversation segued toward a discussion of dog training techniques after that, and before I knew it, the afternoon had waned, and it was time to go home to meet Paisley.

CHAPTER 13

Paisley took to the piano like a duck takes to water. From the first hour, I realized she was a natural. Not only was she able to hear the music, but she seemed to have an ability to sense which keys would create which tones and how those tones would work together to create a melody. She wouldn't need many lessons before she would be ready to move onto more advanced techniques.

"Really being able to read music and to understand all the various symbols might seem sort of boring, and it might seem easier to memorize the keystrokes of whichever song you are trying to play, but it will be important as you become more advanced, so I am going to send a couple of books home with you. I want you to study them, and when you come back on Wednesday, I'm going to quiz you on the first couple of chapters."

"Don't worry." Paisley grinned. "I'll work hard and learn everything you teach me."

I was sure she would. I recognized the same passion in her I'd felt when I'd first been introduced to the piano.

"Will the same time work on Wednesday?" I asked.

"We get out early this Wednesday for teacher planning, so I can come at two if you want."

"That would work well." I remembered that Wednesday was Gracie's bingo night, so maybe I'd invite Cass to grab some dinner or something. I hadn't spoken to him since our encounter yesterday, and I didn't want to let too much time pass in case things had gotten awkward between us. We would be volunteering at the shelter together again tomorrow, which would give me the opportunity to ask him about Wednesday. "Are things getting back to normal now that school has reopened?"

Paisley shrugged. "I guess. Everyone is talking about what happened to Tracy and wondering if the killer is still around and if one of us might be next."

"I bet it is frightening not to know for sure if the sheriff has the real killer in custody."

She nodded. "Some of the kids think the man in the jail is the killer, but a lot of us think they have the wrong person. Tracy didn't even know the man in the campground. Why would he kill her?"

"Sometimes, killings are random, and the victim doesn't know the killer."

"Do you think the man in the jail is the one who killed Tracy?"

"Not really," I answered honestly. "Do you get a ride to and from school?"

She nodded. "My friend, Anna's mom drives me. The principal sent out a letter telling all the parents that it might not be safe to let their children walk until everything is sorted out for sure. It's really scary to think the killer might still be out there."

"Yes, it is," I agreed.

"There are even extra adults monitoring the hallways between classes, and no one is allowed to leave the school grounds without a parent picking them up."

"Haven't you always needed a parent to pick you up if you are going to leave early?"

"No. It used to be a parent could send a note that allowed their kid to get out early and walk home, but not anymore. Now a parent has to come into the office and sign you out."

I figured that was a good policy whether there was a killer lurking about or not.

"Anna said that her older sister, Emma, told her that some of the kids at the middle school think the killer is this creepy guy who hangs out in the field behind the school during lunch break."

"Creepy guy?" I asked, suddenly becoming a whole lot more alert.

"Emma told Anna that this guy hangs out wearing a big coat, waiting for some of the kids who sneak away to talk to him. Emma and Anna's dad told them that he was probably selling drugs and not to go anywhere near him."

"Has anyone told Deputy Wylander about this man?"

Paisley shrugged. "I don't know. Maybe. Emma and Anna's dad talked to the principal in our school, but there wasn't anything he could do because he was far enough away from our school, so he wasn't violating any trespassing rules and no one would admit that he'd tried to sell them drugs or did anything wrong. He just sits there on a rock and watches the kids. Creepy, right?"

"Very creepy. I'll be sure to mention it to Deputy Wylander when I see him. It seems like this man might be a real suspect." I reached down and picked up Alastair, who'd come wandering over. "Do any of the kids ever go talk to him?"

"I don't know. Emma might because she goes to that school."

"Did Emma say if Tracy ever went over to talk to this man?"

Paisley hesitated.

"It could be important," I prompted.

"I don't want to get anyone in trouble."

"Tracy is dead. Nothing you say will get her in trouble. What do you know?"

"I don't know if Tracy talked to the creepy guy in the field, but Emma told Anna and me that Tracy and some of her friends did sneak off campus during lunch to vape. She said they met up with some boys from the high school."

The high school was only a block from the middle school, so I could see how that could happen.

"Do you know the names of any of these boys?"

"No. Emma didn't say."

I supposed I could tell Cass what Paisley had told me and then let him take care of talking to Emma and her parents, but I didn't want to get Emma in any sort of trouble. That wouldn't be fair to Paisley, who'd told me what she had as a friend. Maybe I'd try to get Paisley to point Emma out to me and try to talk to her alone myself. Of course, if I did that, I might be the one to come off looking like the creepy adult who was stalking my ten-year-old neighbor's friends. No, better to tell Cass and let him handle it.

"What is Alastair doing?" Paisley asked.

I turned around to find him pawing at a box. "It looks like he is trying to get at something inside."

Paisley crossed the room and knelt down next to the box. "The label says, 'Halloween Decorations.'"

I smiled. "Maybe Alastair thinks it is time we decorated. Halloween will be here before you know it."

I picked up the box of Christmas decorations on top and set it aside, and then pushed the one with Halloween decorations inside to the center of the room. I opened the lid and pulled out the items on top.

"Cool skeleton," Paisley said. "Can we hang it up?"

"I don't see why not. I think there are some orange lights, fall garlands, and rubber bats in here as well. We may as well do it up right." I continued to dig in and unpack the box onto the floor. "Oh look, my old Inspector Gadget costume."

"Who's Inspector Gadget?"

"A character from a kids' cartoon from the eighties. Basically, he was this klutzy cop or private eye, or maybe he was a spy. Anyway, he was a klutzy guy who had all these cool gadgets that would eventually help him catch the bad guy."

"What kind of gadgets?"

"Weird stuff like a hat that doubled as a helicopter, or mechanical hands with all sorts of attachments. He had a coat that was also a parachute and pants with jet rockets. That sort of thing."

Paisley giggled. "It sounds ridiculous."

"It was, but it was also fun." I set the costume aside. Alastair pounced on it and began to howl. "Sorry, buddy, but the inspector had a dog, not a cat. I think the bad guy was the one who had a cat." I turned to Paisley. "Let's get this stuff downstairs and find a place for it. I think Gracie has some pumpkin-scented candles, and I seem to remember a Halloween wreath for the door. I'll ask her if she still has it." I bent down and started gathering the decorations I'd selected to bring with me. "Oh, and we'll need jack-o'-lanterns before the big night. There used to be a pumpkin patch just down the mountain. Maybe we can go there on Saturday to pick some out."

Paisley's face widened in a smile. "Really? That would be so fun."

"Talk to your grandmother about it, and if it is okay with her, consider it a date. We'll go after my volunteer gig at the Harvest Festival."

CHAPTER 14

Tuesday

"What smells so good?" I asked, coming downstairs with Alastair tagging along behind me.

"Biscuits and sausage gravy. Tom and I are going to a movie this evening, so I won't be making dinner. I decided a big breakfast was just the thing in the event you ended up with a sandwich for dinner."

I'd existed on sandwiches in New York, so I could certainly manage with one for one evening but didn't say as much. "It smells wonderful, and I love your sausage gravy, but you didn't need to go to so much trouble."

Gracie slid a tray of golden biscuits from the oven. "I don't mind. I like a big breakfast sometimes. With the rain and wind and all-around blustery day, it seemed like just the thing."

I poured myself a cup of coffee and sat down at the kitchen counter. "Do you need help?"

"No. I just need to scramble some eggs. I guess you could set the table. Tom will be here as well, so we'll need three place settings."

I took three plates from the cupboard and was just setting them on the table when Tom walked in. He hung his wet hat and jacket in the mudroom, removed his shoes, and then padded into the room in his stocking feet. "Rain's getting harder," he said, pouring his own cup of coffee.

Gracie paused. "Tom dear, could you check the window at the end of the hallway? I opened it just a bit after it stopped raining yesterday and I can't remember if I closed it."

"I'll check." He headed out of the room.

"I hope it's closed," I said, picking out three sets of silverware. "If not, there will be a puddle on the floor."

Gracie stirred the gravy and shrugged. "I have a mop, and the floor has been sealed. If the window was open, the wind might have blown your garland around a bit, though."

"I can fix it. We don't need spoons, do we?"

"No, a knife and fork each will do."

Tom returned to the room. "The window was closed."

"That's good." Gracie smiled at him. "The cream is still in the refrigerator."

He headed in that direction. "I noticed the Halloween decorations. Been a while since anyone put them up here," Tom commented.

"Paisley and I decorated yesterday," I informed him.

"Such a sweet child," Tom said. "Shame about her mother."

"What exactly is wrong with her?" I asked. "Paisley said she was very, very sick, but she didn't mention exactly what ailed her."

"Leukemia," Gracie said. "She's been battling it for a while, although it looks like the dang thing may have won the battle."

I paused and looked up from what I was doing. "Paisley mentioned that she overheard her mom and grandma talking about what will happen when she dies. Tough thing for a kid to overhear."

Gracie glanced at me. "The entire situation is so sad. Not only is the mom basically at death's door, but Ethel has been dealing with health issues as well. I don't know what will happen to that poor child if she decides she is not able to care for her."

"Maybe we can help," I suggested. "With rides, or homework, or even meals."

"That's a good idea," Gracie said. "I'll talk to Ethel to see what she needs help with the most. I would think that transportation might be a biggie. No one is letting their children walk anywhere until they know for sure that Tracy's killer is behind bars."

"I spoke to Paisley about that yesterday." I took a biscuit from the basket Gracie had just placed on the table. They looked delicious, and I was starving. "She said she is being driven to and from school by her friend, Anna's, mother."

"That's good. No child should be on the street alone." Gracie set the gravy on the table, and Tom followed with the eggs, and both joined me.

"Anna has an older sister, Emma, who attends the middle school," I continued. "Paisley told me that Emma told her sister that Tracy and some of her friends would sneak out of school to meet up with some high school boys and vape during lunch."

Gracie frowned. "I don't like to hear that. Does Cass know about it?"

I nodded. "I called him yesterday to fill him in on the vaping and the creepy guy in the field."

"Creepy guy in the field?" Tom asked.

I shared what Paisley had told me about the man who wore a big coat and could possibly be a drug dealer hanging out in the field behind the middle school.

"Someone lurking around the middle school where a child went missing seems like a good lead to me," Tom said.

"I thought so too, but Cass said he already spoke to the guy," I answered. "Apparently, he claims he just likes to sit on the rock and watch the kids. He didn't have any drugs on him when Cass spoke to him, and as far as Cass knew, he hadn't actually approached the school, so he couldn't arrest him for anything. Cass suggested to the man that he might want to find another place to hang out and people watch, but he didn't seem inclined to move, and he was far enough away from the school that Cass couldn't force him to leave. Cass also said he didn't have any reason to believe this guy was the killer, and he has a prosthetic hand. It's a cheap one at that, not the sort you could get a good grip with, and Cass didn't think he would have been able to dig the grave where Tracy was buried."

"He might have had help," Gracie pointed out.

"He might have, and Cass is keeping an eye on him."

"So, what are your plans for today?" Gracie asked, changing the subject.

"I have my first experience as a dog trainer at two, and then Cass and I volunteer from four to six. I thought I might see if he wants to get pizza after that. In the meantime, I'm going to head into town to see if I can get some information from Hope about what exactly is expected of me at the Harvest Festival. The sign-in sheet was sort of vague, and you know I like to be prepared."

"That is true. It did seem like you were two steps ahead of the game most of the time while you were growing up."

Except for forgetting to wear a swimsuit under my clothes on that fateful fishing trip, I reminded myself, still blushing at the memory that refused to fade into the distance now that it had been conjured up. "Paisley and I talked about heading down to the pumpkin patch after my volunteer shift at the Harvest Festival on Saturday. We used to have so much fun picking out pumpkins and eating apple pie. The two of you are welcome to come with us if you'd like."

Gracie looked at Tom. He nodded. "We'd love to come, dear. I'll make a big pot of chili we can heat up and serve when we get back. We'll want to get started on carving those pumpkins, and chili is an easy meal to serve. Remember the year we decided to try our hand at making fancy jack-o'-lanterns using the special knives I bought from the shopping channel?"

I laughed. "Your Charlie Chaplin ended up looking more like Snoopy the dog."

"Poor Charlie did end up with an unfortunate nose." Tom chuckled.

Gracie responded, and I took a minute to sit back and enjoy the banter. I'd missed it yet somehow hadn't even been aware of it until just now. Looking back, I wasn't sure how I'd let myself get so wrapped up in my own life. Fourteen years! I'd been gone for fourteen years and hadn't been back to visit once. Sure, Gracie had come to New York to see me a few times, and there was that one year I had a concert in Chicago and we'd met up there, but to not have come home for more than a decade seemed unimaginable now that I was here, and the memory of what this place had once meant to me was beginning to sink in. When I'd come crawling home a broken and defeated woman, I hadn't planned to stay. I figured I'd lick my wounds and regroup and then find some other dream to chase. But now that I was here, sitting at the family table eating biscuits and gravy while the rain poured down just outside the window, I found myself wondering why on earth I'd ever want to leave. Of course, staying would mean figuring out a way to support myself, and I had no idea what that might be.

"Another biscuit?" Gracie asked me, jogging me from my thoughts.

"No, thank you. This was all delicious." I glanced at Alastair, who was waiting patiently for the bite of egg he knew would be coming. "Alastair and I will get the dishes, and then I'd like to talk to you about some ideas I have for updating my room just a bit."

Gracie looked surprised. "Updating your room? Are you thinking of staying?"

"For now. If that is okay."

Gracie smiled, and I couldn't help but notice the tear in the corner of her eye. "Oh yes, that is more than okay; that is exactly what I've been hoping for."

CHAPTER 15

Hercules was an arrogant little pug who honestly seemed to believe that we'd been paired so that he could train *me*. And maybe that was what was going on. When Naomi first gave him to me to work with on simple commands such as sit and stay, I figured she was starting me off easy. Boy was I wrong.

"Why is it that when I say sit, you jump around, and when I try to walk you on the leash, you sit down and refuse to come along?"

The dog, with his huge brown eyes, just stared at me all innocent, like he had no idea what I was saying. At first, I'd thought the dog somewhat daft, but the longer we worked together, the clearer it became that he was just messing with me.

"I don't outweigh many things, but I outweigh you; now come along." I took several steps toward my goal, dragging the little dog along with me.

"You know that dragging isn't the preferred way of getting a dog to walk on a leash," one of the other trainers said.

"I assumed as much, but this dog is defective. He sits when I tell him to heel and jumps around when I tell him to sit."

The woman laughed. "Hercules does have a mind of his own, but he's been through the basics and knows what to do if motivated to do so. May I?" She held out her hand, and I passed her Hercules's leash. She took a small treat out of her fanny pack, making sure the dog saw it. She then told him to heel and started walking, holding the treat just out of his reach. After they'd traveled across the room, she paused, told the dog to sit, and gave him the treat.

"Ah, so that's what those little pieces of meat are for."

"Didn't Naomi show you what to do?" the woman asked.

"She was going to, but then she got a call about one of the goats being stuck in the fence and had to leave to deal with that. She told me to wait for her, but Hercules and I got tired of waiting, so we decided to get started. I thought I knew what to do. I was wrong." I glanced down at the dog. "You know he is evil? I could tell he knew exactly what to do but refused to do it anyway."

"You let Hercules think he was the alpha in this situation. Jasper and I are going to work on sit/stay and recall. Why don't you and Hercules work with us today? That way, I can help you if you forget what to do."

"That would be great," I said with relief. "I'm Callie."

"I'm Willa. Is this your first day?"

I nodded. "I guess that is obvious. I thought I understood what to do, but I guess I was wrong about that as well."

"Don't worry. Hercules is a smart dog. Once he understands that you are the boss, he'll cooperate."

Willa showed me how to hold the treat just over the dog's head to prompt sitting behavior when Hercules refused to do it. The tiny bites of meat seemed to work wonders in terms of getting him to do what I wanted him to do, but I had to wonder if the dog's new owner was going to have to walk around with treats in his pocket all the time.

"No, the dogs are weaned off the treats once they learn the behavior," Willa explained after I asked that question. "Initially, the dogs are put through short training sessions and rewarded every time. Once they seem to understand the behavior we are asking them to demonstrate, we ask them to demonstrate the behavior twice before they get a treat. Eventually, we require more and more demonstrations of the behavior before a treat is presented until eventually, they will happily do as you ask without the treats being offered. In fact, many of the dogs enjoy a few minutes of play or a hearty neck scruff as a reward even more than a treat. After you work with the dogs for a while, you'll begin to have a feel for which dogs prefer to play, which want hugs and kisses, and which are little piggies like Hercules, here, and prefer food over anything else."

"Aren't you afraid he'll get fat?"

"Naomi monitors all the dogs' weights. The treats are high quality and are taken into account when calculating their daily food allotment."

I glanced at Hercules, who was sitting next to Jasper, waiting for his recall command like some sort of sweet little angel. I glared at him to let him know I was on to him, but he just smiled at me with his sweet little pug eyes, letting me know that he had my number and the battle between us was far from over.

Hercules's part of the session came to an end seemingly as soon as it got started. Willa and I traded out dogs, and next, I was paired with a sweet golden retriever who looked at me with love and adoration and tried very hard to anticipate all my needs. Now, this was the dog for me, I decided. Docile and sweet and willing to please.

The two-hour session seemed to fly by, and before I knew it, I was saying goodbye to Willa and hello to Cass, who had shown up for his volunteer time. This shift was focused on play rather than training, so I let Cass select the dogs and outline the plan, while I went along for the ride. With all the rain, we decided on an indoor session and, as we had before, gathered ropes and balls and headed to the large play area.

"So how was your first one-on-one training session?" Cass asked after we'd organized the dogs we'd chosen to spend time with.

"It started off rocky when I was paired with a pug with an attitude but one of the other trainers, Willa, helped me out and things went fine from there."

"Willa has been volunteering for a long time. She is a good one to go to for help if Naomi isn't around.

Where is Naomi anyway? She usually pops in to say hi."

"She had a goat emergency. One of them got stuck in a fence."

Cass frowned. "That doesn't sound good."

I frowned as well. "Naomi has been gone for a long time. Do you think we should check on her? I just assumed she had everything under control."

"I'll call her cell." Cass took out his phone and punched in a number.

I couldn't hear everything that was being said from her end, but it sounded like Naomi was with the vet, who was trying to patch up the animal, who'd suffered some fairly significant injuries during his encounter with the fence.

Cass hung up and looked at me. "Naomi will be held up for a while yet. I told her we'd see to the feeding and end-of-day tucking in when we are done here. Or at least I will if you have to go."

"I can stay. What do we do?"

"Naomi has instructions for each animal in terms of the type and amount of food to be presented at each meal pinned to the board in her office. We'll just need to distribute the food, check everyone's water supply, clean up any messes we come across along the way and make sure everyone is tucked in and locked up for the night. It will take a couple hours, less with two of us working, but it isn't hard. Maybe we can grab a pizza after."

I bent down to hug a terrier who'd come over to say hello. "That sounds wonderful. I'm not sure I've had pizza since I left home."

"They don't have pizza in New York?"

"Of course they do. Really good pizza from what I understand. But I lived a busy life after I left here, so I usually just grabbed a sandwich or a piece of fruit. Something I could eat while I drove from one place to the next."

"No wonder you are so skinny. Pizza is the elixir of life. I make sure to have one at least once a week."

I was about to warn Cass that he was going to get fat, but one look at his flat stomach and broad chest informed me that he was far from overweight. I supposed that if one got enough exercise, a pizza a week wouldn't kill you.

I bent down and picked up a ball and tossed it. Five dogs took off after it. "I meant to ask if you've made any progress on Tracy Porter's murder."

"I can't say I've made significant progress, but I have been working on it," Cass replied. "I received the timesheets for all three suspects from the substitute pool, and it looks like Veronica Jones, at least, is off the hook. While she was at the middle school when Tracy disappeared, her teaching assignments did not line up with either Stella's or Hillary's disappearances. Harvey Underwood, however, was at all three schools at the time the girls disappeared, so he has moved up on my list."

"And the creepy janitor?"

"He was assigned to the middle school here in town when both Stella and Tracy went missing, but he was not working in Rivers Bend when Hillary disappeared. In fact, he was assigned to Foxtail Lake High School at that time. If we are operating on the assumption that the same person killed all three girls, it couldn't have been him."

"So what does that leave you with? Have you pared down your list outside of the three subs?"

"I will admit that my list is thin. Very thin. If I look at Tracy's murder in isolation, I can come up with a fistful of suspects, but most of the people who would be on that list didn't even live here twenty years ago. While I understand that it appears as if these three girls were killed by the same person, I think I'm going to need to widen my parameters if I am going to track down Tracy's killer."

"But you are still looking at Underwood?"

"Very much so."

"And the homeless guy? Buck Darwin. What is going on with him?"

"He is in custody awaiting trial. As I said before, he hasn't done a thing to clear himself, but he hasn't pled guilty either. He seems to be in some sort of a holding pattern. I almost feel that by pleading no contest, he is waiting for something to happen."

"Like what?"

"I wish I knew. It just seems that he is working really hard to stay in the neutral zone between declaring either guilt or innocence. The whole thing is rather odd."

"Okay, so at this point you have a man in custody who neither of us thinks is guilty yet hasn't done a thing to prove his innocence, and a substitute teacher with opportunity but no apparent motive. Is that really it?"

"So far."

"What about the creepy man Paisley told me about?"

"Craig Grainger. He is still on my list, but I don't see how he could have strangled Tracy and then buried her in the grave with only one functional hand."

I guess Cass had a point. It would be hard to strangle a person or dig a grave with only one hand. I know I had a hard time doing many of the simple chores I once had. "So unless this Harvey Underwood did kill Stella, Hillary, and Tracy, you have no viable suspects because I am going to assume Buck Darwin was not around Foxtail Lake when Stella died."

"As far as I know, he wasn't, but like I said, he isn't talking. He isn't from around here, but I suppose a drifter could move in and out of a particular area over time, so it is possible he was in Colorado both ten and twenty years ago."

As soon as playtime was over, we headed to Naomi's office to check the menu for each animal and begin preparing the meals. We fed the dogs, cats, puppies, and kittens first, and then moved on to the larger animals. Cass seemed to be on a first-name basis with every animal living at the facility. I wasn't sure why, but I found that endearing.

Once everyone was fed and tucked in, Cass and I headed toward our favorite pizza place.

"I've been wanting a Froggy's Pizza ever since I've been home," I said as we slipped into a booth in the back.

"Best pizza in town," Cass agreed. "Are you still a cheese-only purist?"

"I think I am. But if you want toppings, we can do half and half."

"Actually," Cass answered, "I like cheese. Beer? Wine?"

"I wouldn't mind a glass of wine."

"Red or white?"

"Red. Cabernet or whatever the house special is."

Cass got up to place our order, and I sat back and took in the ambience. As many of the businesses in town had, Froggy's had gone all out with Halloween decorations. Spiders hung from fake cobwebs attached to the ceiling, fake jack-o'-lanterns with built-in lights had been placed randomly around the room, and a giant Frankenstein greeted customers as they walked in the front door. When I'd lived here years ago, a man named Fred Parker had owned the place. I wondered if he still did. Fred had seemed old fourteen years ago. I figured by now he must be at least sixty-five, or maybe even seventy.

I looked up as Cass approached with a beer for him and glass of wine for me. He set them on the table and then slid into the booth. "They'll bring the pizza out when it's ready."

"I've been admiring the decorations."

"Fred always does the holidays up big."

"So he still owns the place?"

Cass nodded. "His grandson, Trevor, runs the place day-to-day, but Fred is very much still around, lurking in the background, keeping an eye on things."

"So it didn't work out with his son taking over?"

Cass shook his head. "Brian had other plans and moved away shortly after you did. Trevor is only twenty-one, but he seems to really want to take over the business and has worked hard to prove that he's up for it. Fred hovered over his shoulder to a degree that would make me want to shoot him during the first couple of years, but he seems to have mellowed a bit now. He still pops in, but usually only to make his presence felt, and then he leaves."

"Is Brian's sister, Jessica, still around?"

"She is," Cass answered, and then frowned.

"Is something wrong?" I asked.

"It just occurred to me that Jessica is someone I should talk to about Tracy's disappearance. I'm not sure why her name hasn't come up before."

"Jessica knew Tracy?"

He nodded. "Jessica used to work at the hair salon with Tracy's mom. She quit a few years ago, finished her degree, and took a job as a guidance counselor. She works two days a week at the middle school and three days a week at the high school. I hadn't thought about it, but she was working at the high school when I interviewed the middle school staff, so I never did talk to her. As a counselor and a friend of the family, she might very well have useful insights into what was going on in Tracy's life when she disappeared." He smiled at me. "Thanks for the prompt."

"My pleasure," I answered, even though I hadn't done anything. "Are you thinking the attack on Tracy was personal rather than random?"

Cass pursed his lips. "I'm not sure. But I am sure that if I am going to solve this case, I am going to need to turn over every rock I can, and interviewing Jessica is a rock I should have turned over a while ago."

It seemed to me that Cass was being overly hard on himself, but he had always been that way. I think the fact that we both shared a certain intensity is what had gotten us to be friends in the first place. There were other ways Cass and I were alike too. He was a bit more of an extrovert than I was, but we both worked hard and took our responsibilities seriously. That night, as we chatted and laughed, I found myself wondering why he'd never married. He seemed like exactly the sort of husband most women would want: kind, dependable, and oh so good-looking. The fact that he hadn't settled down and started a family suddenly struck me as very odd indeed.

CHAPTER 16

Wednesday

When I woke the next morning to hear that another girl had been found in a shallow grave similar to the one in which Tracy had been buried, everyone assumed the same killer was responsible for both deaths. I wasn't so sure. Yes, I got the fact that it was unlikely there were two killers running around in one small town isolated way up in the mountains, but while there were things that tied the girls together, there were also things that distinguished the most recent killing as being different from the previous three already identified.

For one thing, Patricia Long was a high school student while Stella, Hillary, and Tracy had been in middle school. For another, while Patricia did have scratches on her face, according to Cass, who'd texted me a brief message first thing that morning, they were shallow, as if they'd been made by fingernails, while the tears in the skin of the other three were deep, as if inflicted by a wild animal or some sort of clawlike tool. Both Tracy and Patricia had been found in a shallow grave in the same part of the woods, but the location of the former's gravesite, and the fact that Tracy had suffered from claw marks, were well known by everyone in town, so the possibility that Patricia had been killed by a copycat was a very good possibility in my mind.

The one positive thing to come from this second murder was that it forced the mayor and the sheriff to take a step back from their assurance that Buck Darwin was to blame for Tracy's death. As far as I knew, he hadn't yet been released from jail, but I wouldn't be a bit surprised if that didn't happen at some point in the day.

"I guess you heard?" Gracie said when I wandered out into the yard where she was helping Tom hang the white lights from the eaves of the house that I remembered her putting up every fall when I was growing up. She'd leave them there through the winter until the longer days of late spring returned.

"I heard. Did you know this girl?" I asked.

"Not really. I think her family moved to town at the beginning of the school year last year. I spoke to Ida, who told me that Patricia was a seventeen-year-old high school senior, and she'd actually been missing since Saturday."

"Saturday? Why didn't Cass know about that before now?" I asked.

"According to Ida, who lives across the street from the family, so she knows them quite well, Patricia was last seen going out on a date on Saturday evening. It seems her parents didn't care for the boy she was dating, and they argued before she left. When their daughter didn't come home that night, they assumed she was off on one of her snits."

"Snits?"

"I guess Patricia was prone to episodes when she would get angry and disappear for a few days and then show up after she'd worked through the drama of the moment," Gracie said. "Or at least that's the way Ida put it. It wasn't the first time she'd taken off, so when she didn't come home on Sunday, as she was supposed to, her parents didn't think much of it. When she didn't show up for school on Monday or Tuesday, they began calling around to her friends, but no one said they had seen her. It wasn't until late last night that they finally called Cass. Patricia's mother had a bad dream she described as prophetic. On a hunch, Cass and Milo searched the same area where Tracy's body was discovered and found Patricia buried there as well."

"I didn't talk to Cass this morning; he texted me, and his message was brief, but he did say that it looked as if the victim had been dead for a few days."

"Ida indicated that she'd heard something similar," Gracie confirmed.

Tom climbed down the ladder because Gracie had stopped feeding him lights. He pulled off his gloves and slapped them together. "I heard on the scanner that the sheriff is linking Tracy and Patricia's deaths as being carried out by the same individual."

"I heard that as well," I confirmed. "While there are similarities, I'm not so sure, though. I think it's possible that someone else could have killed this poor girl, and then made it look as if she'd been killed by the same person to divert suspicion." I went on to compare the two murders, pointing out the differences as well as the similarities.

"If the killer is a copycat, I think I'd want to have a long chat with the boyfriend," Tom said.

I looked out toward the lake. Other than a slight breeze rippling the surface, the weather was fairly calm today. I missed the geese that made Foxtail Lake their home in the summer, but I didn't blame them for flying south before the first real freeze set in. "The boyfriend seems like an obvious choice as the killer. The two had been out on a date. I supposed there are all sorts of things teenagers do when they go out on a weekend evening. Many drink and some even do drugs. It does seem like a recipe for disaster. Still, the boyfriend as the killer seems too obvious."

"This isn't a movie," Gracie pointed out. "It is a real-life situation, and the obvious choice is usually the correct one. Unlike in a novel, where a twist might be assumed."

I shrugged. "I suppose you're right. Still, my intuition tells me that the boyfriend won't turn out to be the killer."

"Cass might have some insight into what happened on Saturday after Patricia left her home," Gracie said. "If you are still going out this evening, I suppose you can ask him."

"Oh, I will. In the meantime, I'm going to help you hang the lights and then I'm going to give Paisley her piano lesson. Are you still going to bingo tonight?"

"I am. I won't be late. If your plans with Cass fall through, there is plenty of food in the refrigerator."

I picked up a string of lights and began draping one of the large shrubs that grew along the front of the house. I'd once asked Gracie why she left the lights up from October through April, and she'd told me that winters in the Rockies could be long, dark, and bitterly cold; a little bit of sparkle was just the thing to lift your spirits at a time when you needed it.

CHAPTER 17

If anyone had told me even a week earlier that I would be looking forward to giving a piano lesson, I would have said they were nuts. After my accident, I hadn't thought I'd ever find joy in music again, but Paisley's enthusiasm was infectious, and I found myself humming the melody of the simple song I planned to teach her today. In many ways, teaching Paisley to experience the magic of the piano helped me to remember what it had been like for me to experience the wonder of music for the first time. When had I let attention to the mechanics replace the joy I'd once experienced as my fingers flowed over the ivory keys? I suppose the enchantment I'd found as a child had drifted away at about the same time I'd decided to take my passion to the next level, to carve out a career from what had once been a hobby.

"Callie, are you here?" I heard Paisley call from downstairs.

I glanced at the clock. She was early. She must have let herself in. "I'm up in the attic," I called back.

I heard the pounding of footsteps on the stairs as she made her way up.

"You're early."

Paisley bent down to greet Alastair, who'd trotted over to say hello. "I asked Anna's mom to drop me off here rather than going home first and walking over. I hope that's okay."

"That's fine as long as your grandmother knows what you are doing."

"She knows." Paisley walked farther into the room. "I called her from Anna's mom's phone. She wondered if you could give me a ride home. She doesn't want me out walking around by myself after what happened to that girl from the high school."

"I'll be happy to drive you home, and I agree with your grandmother. No walking outside without an adult until whoever is killing girls is caught. Agreed?"

Paisley nodded. "Agreed." She crossed the room and sat down on the piano bench. "I've studied the books you gave me if you want to quiz me."

"That's great. Why don't you tell me what you learned?"

She opened to a piece of sheet music and went down the row, calling out the notes.

"That's very good," I said. "You are a fast learner."

"I would be even faster if I had a piano to practice on at home."

"Perhaps a keyboard."

"A keyboard?" Paisley asked.

"It's like a piano, only it is just the keys. It won't give you the same quality of tone as a piano, but it is great for practicing. Of course, you'd need to wear headphones, so you won't disturb your mother and grandmother."

Paisley's eyes grew big. "That sounds awesome. Do you have one?"

"No," I admitted. "But there is a shop in town where we can probably get one. Let's call your grandmother to make sure it is okay for you to have it. If it is, we'll go buy one for you to take home and maybe just have a shorter lesson today."

"Okay. I'll call her." Paisley grinned.

As it turned out, Paisley's grandmother was more than okay with her granddaughter having a keyboard as long as it came with headphones so she would not disturb her mother's rest. Shopping with the enthusiastic ten-year-old was the most fun I'd had in a very long time. We not only purchased a keyboard and headphones but a selection of sheet music for beginners too. By the time we had tried out all the different options and made our selection, it was getting late, and Paisley admitted to having homework, so I took her home and arranged to give her a lesson the following day.

CHAPTER 18

The restaurant Cass had chosen was nice but casual, unlike the elegance of the steak house the previous week. I was glad I'd decided on slacks rather than a dress. I didn't want to appear overdressed any more than I wanted to appear underdressed. Not that Cass would care what I was wearing one way or another, but life in the Big Apple had made me a bit more conscientious about my attire than I'd been when I'd lived in Foxtail Lake as a teen.

"Didn't this used to be a pancake house?"

"It was. Grizzly's was open for breakfast and lunch only seasonally, from the beginning of May through the end of September, when the campground and cabins were open. Then, about five years ago, the place was sold, and the new owner opens year-round, but only for dinner."

"There used to be big, family-size booths rather than these tables and chairs, and the gas fireplace in the corner used to be a wood stove."

Cass nodded. "The new owner wanted to upgrade the interior, so he stripped it down to the studs and rebuilt. The log exterior is the same, and the food, while different, is as good as it always was."

"What do you usually get?" I asked, picking up the menu.

"Sometimes I go for a burger or sandwich. They're all good, and the portions are large. But my favorite is the beef stew and corn bread. You can always take your leftovers home for lunch tomorrow if you can't finish whatever you choose."

I set the menu aside. "Beef stew sounds perfect. And I'll have a glass of wine and a glass of water to drink."

Cass waved to the waiter and placed our order. When he left to fetch our beverages, I asked Cass about this most recent murder case. I knew that bringing up such a gruesome subject at dinner might not be proper etiquette, but I'd been curious all day and couldn't wait to get some answers.

"As I briefly mentioned in my text, Patricia Long was a seventeen-year-old high school student who was last seen by her parents on Saturday evening, when she left for a date with her boyfriend, Rich Cutter. Apparently, Patricia's parents were not a fan of the boy Patricia had been dating, and they argued before she left. When she didn't come home when expected, they figured she'd taken off on one of her classic cooling-off periods. When she wasn't home by last night, they called me. On a hunch, I took Milo to look in the same area of the forest where Tracy's remains were found the previous week and found Patricia buried not far away."

"I take it you've spoken to the boyfriend?"

Cass nodded. "He took Patricia to a party, and the two argued while they were there. He claimed that Patricia had been moody all evening and he just wanted to relax and have fun, so he left her chatting with friends while he went outside to smoke pot with some of the guys. Based on what multiple partygoers have told me, it seems Patricia found fault in his choice and let him know it. He told me he snapped back about not wanting to deal with her mood swings and she left."

"Left the party?"

"As far as I can tell, yes. According to Rich, she stormed back into the house, but no one I have spoken to who was at the party remembers seeing her coming back inside after she went out to confront Rich. I figure either Patricia left the party at that point or Rich is lying and he left with her but didn't want me to know that because he killed her."

"Did anyone remember seeing Rich back inside after Patricia went out to confront him?" I wondered.

"Yes, but most of the kids I spoke to were unclear on the timeline. Some were under the impression he was at the party the whole time, while others were certain that he left and then returned."

"So he could have left, killed Patricia, and then returned to the party?"

"Exactly. Based on what I've been able to unravel, most if not all of the teens in attendance were drinking and smoking pot. The witness statements I've collected have been so varied as to be worthless. What I do know is that it seems possible to me that the boyfriend left the party, killed Patricia, buried her in a shallow grave, and then went back to the party. His only alibi is his presence there, but because no one really seems certain whether he was there the entire time or if he left and came back, his story isn't much of an alibi."

"Did he have blood on his clothes? In his car? There must have been blood if he killed her."

"I didn't find any clothing with blood on it in his home, but he could have disposed of the soiled articles had there been any. His car is clean, but he could very well have killed Patricia after they arrived at the burial site. It makes sense to me that Rich might have been drunk and stoned and killed her in a fit of rage, but my instinct is that he isn't the killer. I'll just follow the evidence and see where I end up."

I smiled at the waiter when he brought our drinks. He seemed very nice and even took the time to provide the history of the wine I'd be sampling even though I'd simply ordered the house wine. After he left, I continued the conversation. "So if the boyfriend is not your guy, any clue to who might have done it?"

Cass took a sip of his beer before answering. "I've spent the entire day interviewing the kids who attended the party, as well as Patricia's family and other classmates. Three people stood out as having both motive and opportunity in addition to Rich. Gayleen Hamilton was one of Patricia's best friends, at least until recently. It seems that Gayleen and Rich used to date until she walked in on Rich and Patricia in a bedroom at a party several weeks ago."

"Ouch."

"Ouch is right. According to the teens I spoke to who were friends of both Patricia and Gayleen, the situation between them became extremely explosive. Gayleen keyed Patricia's car, and Patricia retaliated by taking a can of spray paint to the mural Gayleen had created in the quad at the high school. Both girls seem to have been actively participating in an ongoing war that had left their other friends on edge. When Patricia showed up at the party with Rich, the kids who were with Gayleen said that she went a little bit nuts and vowed to take care of 'the backstabbing witch' once and for all."

"It definitely sounds like she had a motive," I commented.

"It does. I couldn't find a single partygoer who would admit to seeing Patricia and Gayleen together, though, so I have no proof that Gayleen might have followed through with her threat to take care of her nemesis in a permanent manner, but I'm still working on that."

I took a sip of my wine. It was a local brand with which I was unfamiliar, and very good, just as the waiter had promised. I'd have to find out where I could buy some.

"You said you had three suspects other than Rich."

"Suspect number two is a teacher at the high school. He is a first-year teacher who very unwisely showed up at the party attended by his students. According to some of the other teens at the party, it seemed as if Patricia and this teacher have been engaged in a flirtation of sorts. He assured me that his relationship with all his students is nothing but professional, but I'm not convinced of that."

"I agree that you should have your suspicions. If he did have only a teacher/student relationship with the kids, why would he be at the party in the first place?"

"I agree. His denial of any sort of inappropriate behavior is suspect in my book. I'm following up on things, and I still have others to speak to, including his peers at the school. I don't know for certain whether he is involved in Patricia's death, but I can imagine a scenario in which, if he did have an inappropriate relationship with a student, he could have killed her to protect his secret."

"Sure. That makes sense. And suspect number three?"

"A student named Walter Young, who was at the party but had not been invited. According to some of Patricia's friends, Walter was obsessed with Patricia, who was a very pretty girl. Some of the students I spoke to even went so far as to say that Walter was stalking Patricia, which was the reason he was at the party."

"And what does Walter have to say about that?"

"I haven't been able to track him down yet, but I will."

We paused our conversation when the waiter delivered our salads. We both must have been hungry because it seemed that there was some sort of mutual agreement between us that we eat them before we began to speak again. It sounded like Cass had four solid suspects in this case, but none of them would probably come into play if Cass could establish a link to Tracy's murder. I was curious to see what he thought about that. I was also curious to find out what the sheriff thought and how that would affect Tracy's case. The man who was still being held in custody for that murder couldn't possibly have killed Patricia.

The waiter picked up our salad plates and delivered our entrées, and I asked Cass what he thought about a connection between the two most recent murder cases.

"Honestly, I will be surprised if there turns out to be a single killer. While there are similarities, they seem intentional. I suspect a copycat."

"I think so as well. It almost looks as if the killer duplicated the details that have been publicized in Tracy's death to make it seem like the same person killed both girls. What does the sheriff think?"

Cass paused to take a bite of his stew before he commented. "The sheriff is in a tough spot. On the one hand, he has already publicly announced that Buck Darwin killed Tracy. Buck was in custody when Patricia was killed, so we know he couldn't have killed her; by taking a stand that the two murders are related, he would basically be admitting he was wrong about Buck in the first place. On the other hand, if he comes out and says that the two deaths appear not to be connected, he is saving face with Buck, all the while informing people that we have not one but two killers in our community. Either way, I think he is screwed in terms of instilling confidence in his abilities in the people who voted him into office."

"Is Buck still in custody?"

"For now. The sheriff is going to have to take some sort of action and either come out in favor of or against the one-killer theory by tomorrow, I would think. It will be interesting to see how he handles things. Would you like dessert?"

I sat back in my chair. "No, thanks. I'm stuffed. I will take a to-go box, as you suggested. You were correct when you said the leftover stew would make a wonderful lunch."

"So, how did Paisley's piano lesson go?" Cass asked, seemingly from out of the blue. I supposed he might want to talk about something other than work.

"She seems like a natural. She didn't have a way to practice at home, so I bought her a keyboard and a pair of headphones."

"That was nice of you. I remember that you used to have a keyboard that you would bring around when the two of us practiced our songs for the band we talked about creating but never got around to. Maybe you could have just given that one to her and saved yourself the outlay."

"I think Gracie got rid of that old thing a long time ago. It was never the same after it fell on the floor and the frame cracked. Paisley seemed thrilled with her gift, and it didn't cost all that much. Besides, I lived very frugally for a lot of years and managed to put away a nice nest egg, so I can afford to buy a gift for my friends every now and then."

Cass chuckled. "Good to know. I need a new truck."

"Not that kind of gift," I countered. "Besides, every time I've seen you since I've been back, you've been driving an official sheriff's vehicle."

"That's because my truck is in the shop. Again. The poor thing has served me well, but she's getting tired. I know I should break down and buy a new one, but every time I think I've made the decision to trade her in, I find myself fixing her instead."

"That's because you are a loyal and sentimental guy. The fact that you value the people and things you have in your life is one of the things I find the most endearing about you."

"Endearing?" Cass grinned.

"Don't get a big head; I find a lot of people endearing." I glanced at the check the waiter had left on the table. "Are you ready?"

"I am. Just let me pay this, and we'll be on our way."

The ride back to Gracie's was a mostly silent one until a thought occurred to me. "You said that Patricia had scratch marks on her face the same as Tracy, but they weren't as deep. Do you know if they were delivered pre- or postmortem?"

"The medical examiner said it appeared that the scratch marks were delivered after the victim was already dead, and while they penetrated the skin, they didn't go so deep as to penetrate bone, the way the claw marks on Stella and Tracy's face had."

"And what about Tracy's claw wounds? Were they pre- or postmortem?"

"It is hard to know for certain when the marks were delivered because Tracy's remains were partially decayed. I pulled the files for both Stella and Hillary. In both those cases, like Tracy, the remains were decayed, so whether the marks were delivered before or after death could not be ascertained, but in all three cases the scratches were deep, and it was determined they were caused by a tool of some sort."

CHAPTER 19

Friday

By the time my volunteer session with Naomi had rolled around again, Buck had been released from jail, and the manhunt was on for the person the sheriff was assuring everyone was responsible for both Tracy and Patricia's deaths. Cass and I were both convinced we were looking for two separate killers, but for the time being, we decided to keep that opinion to ourselves. Well, at least mostly to ourselves. I'd discussed the situation with Gracie and Tom over dinner the night before, and when I ran into Hope at the farmers market, the two of us had discussed the various possibilities as well.

"It won't be long now," I said to Alastair. Neither of us could sleep, so we'd snuck up into the attic to sit in the window and watch the sun rise over the distant mountain peak. I could still remember sitting in this same window as a child, watching the sun rise and wondering what the day would bring.

"I received an email from the music studio that had offered me a teaching position after the accident. I thanked them for the offer but turned them down. I've enjoyed working with Paisley, but I don't think I want to teach piano for a living. I think it would feel too much like I was living on the outskirts of my old life. What I need," I picked up the cat and hugged him to my chest, "is to totally remake my life." I leaned against the wall behind me. Alastair purred loudly as I spoke to him. "I'm considering moving back to Foxtail Lake permanently. I wasn't sure I'd want to stay here when I first came schlepping home, but I do think I could be happy here. In New York, all I really have are the ashes of my old life, but here I have you and Gracie, and Tom too, of course. I have Paisley and the animal shelter, and then there's Cass. We were close once, and I feel like we can be close again."

I closed my eyes and let my mind drift back over the years. Cass and me building a fort, which Stella thought was dumb until it was finished and she could see how totally cool it actually was. Cass and me fishing and hiking, making plans for the future, and creating music in his garage while his parents were at work. Stella had been my best friend, but in reality, Cass and I were more alike. The bond between us had always been strong, but after Stella died, our friendship seemed to mature into something that was much more.

Why on earth had I ever let us lose touch?

I opened my eyes and set the cat down beside me. The first rays of light brightened the horizon. "It looks like we are in for a red sky. Given all the clouds, I'm not surprised."

"Meow."

"Yes, I do enjoy a moody sky. Skies that are bright and sunny are nice now and then, but a sky filled with clouds is so much more interesting."

As the sun made its first appearance over the horizon, I let my thoughts drift to the two murder cases Cass was tackling. Going against the grain and looking for two killers when the sheriff had already assured the community there was only one was not going to be easy. Not if he wanted to keep his job at least.

There were two other deputies assigned to the Foxtail Lake office. Rafe Conaway was just a few years away from retirement. I was sort of surprised they hadn't made him lead deputy when Quinby retired because he'd been with the department for a lot longer than Cass, but perhaps he hadn't wanted the extra responsibility. I remembered Conaway as being an okay guy, but I suspected that by this time he was just putting in his time and wouldn't want to make any waves.

Trent Vinton was the second deputy assigned to work with Cass. I'd never met him, but Cass had told me that he was a young officer on his first assignment who was just putting in his time until he was offered a chance to move on to a better position.

In a way, I felt bad for Cass. It didn't seem as if either of his crew was looking to put in the effort necessary to be much help. Short-timers generally didn't commit the time and energy needed to find the answers to solve cases as complex as the ones Cass was dealing with.

Uncrossing my legs and setting my feet on the floor, I looked around for the cat, who'd jumped down while I was mulling over the clues Cass had come up with in my mind.

"Alastair?"

"Meow."

I got up and crossed the room to find the cat with his head in a box.

I smiled. "What did you find, you silly cat?"

"Meow." He pulled his head out of the box and looked at me.

"I hope we don't have mice. Aunt Gracie loves all things big and small, but mice indoors are not her favorite combination."

"Meow." Alastair stuck his head in the small opening he'd worked on creating, which would allow his head but not his body inside.

I slit the tape and opened the box the rest of the way. It was filled with old books. Paperbacks, hardbacks, yearbooks, even handwritten journals. I picked up the journal on the top of the pile and opened it slowly. I'd forgotten all about this. After Stella was murdered, Aunt Gracie had taken me to see a counselor who'd asked me to write down my thoughts in a journal every night before I went to bed. At the time, I thought the chore silly and unhelpful, but looking back, writing down the fear, sadness, and hopelessness I'd felt had really helped.

"'Day one,'" I read aloud. "'My stupid shrink told me to write in this stupid book every stupid day, and Aunt Gracie asked me to please cooperate, but this whole thing is really dumb. Stella is dead. Puking out my thoughts is not going to bring her back. Everyone seems to think I am sad, but what I am is angry. I'm angry that Stella is gone. I'm angry that Stella was stupid enough to walk home alone just because she was mad at me. I'm angry there is a monster out there who killed my best friend and might kill me. And I'm angry everyone keeps asking me whether or not I'm okay. Of course, I'm not okay. How could I be?'"

I looked at the cat. "I remember the anger. I remember the fear and guilt that fueled that anger."

"Meow."

Alastair rubbed his body against mine, purring loudly as if to offer comfort. I skipped through the journal until I'd reached the middle. I read the page I'd landed on. "'I heard Aunt Gracie talking. She was telling Tom that the deputies had found blood in an old deserted barn. They think the blood is Stella's blood. They think the site they found is the actual location where Stella was murdered.'"

I looked up from the journal and tried to remember back. I remembered that the deputy in charge had determined that the location where Stella had been buried had not been the place where she'd been murdered. It seemed to me that she'd gone missing from the school, or somewhere between the school and her home, but she'd been murdered more than a mile from there and buried clear across the lake. I hadn't stopped to think about the logistics of the whole thing. If the killer had moved her twice, he must have had a vehicle with him when he grabbed her. Could she have known him? Could someone have offered her a ride and she'd accepted?

Deciding to retrace the path taken by the killer, I stood up, taking the journal with me, and headed to my room to dress. The plan that was forming in my mind was to walk the path between the school and Stella's home and try to identify probable locations where she might have been taken by someone in a car without anyone seeing what had happened. I then thought I'd drive out to the deserted farm where it was determined Stella most likely had been killed, and finally, I'd drive out to the place where her remains had been found. It had been twenty years, and I was under no illusion that there would be any clues to find at any of these places, but maybe by retracing the path of the killer, I'd be able to gain some insight into exactly what had gone through the guy's mind. At least I was assuming it was a guy. I somehow couldn't picture a woman doing to Stella what had been done to her. Perhaps once I'd gone through all that, I'd call Cass to see if he'd found the location where Tracy had been murdered. If he had, perhaps I'd try the same exercise, retracing the steps her killer might have taken on the day she died. Again, I didn't necessarily think I'd find anything, but somehow it seemed like an important step to take.

CHAPTER 20

When I'd called Cass to share my plans, he'd offered to come along with me on my little field trip. I suspected he'd already done what I was proposing to do, but perhaps he'd figured having a pair of fresh eyes on the trek couldn't hurt.

"According to the report I pulled from the file, the deputy who responded to Stella's missing persons report determined from interviews with other students that she must have left school via this footpath."

Cass and I stood at the beginning of a footpath that ran from the back of the baseball field through the woods and out to the street that ran parallel to the school.

"Aspen Drive?"

Cass nodded. "If you turn right on Aspen Drive, it meanders along but eventually intersects with Oak

Avenue after about half of a mile. I'm sure you remember that Stella lived on Oak Avenue."

"I remember. I would walk with Stella to her house almost every day, and Aunt Gracie would pick me up there." I turned and glanced back toward the middle school parking lot, which was full on a Friday morning. "We didn't usually take this path, however. Most of the time we'd just follow the drive from the parking area to Willow Lane, which intersected with Oak Avenue in half the time it took to walk this way." I found myself frowning. "I wonder why she took this path, especially if she was alone. There would have been a lot of other kids walking in the same direction if she had stayed on the road."

"I don't know," Cass admitted. "I wish I did. All I know is that the deputy who investigated the murder determined that Stella was last seen taking this path alone."

I took a few steps forward and glanced down the narrow path, which was almost completely concealed under a canopy of trees, giving it a desolate and isolated feel. "Do you think she was abducted while on the path?"

"Again, I don't know. The deputy who investigated didn't know either. What I do know is that this little path ends on a section of Aspen Drive that wasn't populated. If Stella wasn't abducted from the path, she may have found someone waiting on the road when she emerged. That idea is supported by the fact that she appears to have been transported prior to being killed."

"The deserted farm where she was killed."

Cass nodded. "Aspen Drive eventually connects to County Road 12 if you turn left rather than right when you emerge from these woods. County Road 12 would be the one you'd take to get to the barn where the blood that was confirmed to be Stella's was found. It was the opinion of the deputy who led the investigation at that time that was where she was killed. I agree with him."

"Can I see the barn?"

"It was torn down, and the land it sat on was purchased by the conservancy."

That would be the local land conservancy that was committed to buying up sensitive land and returning it to its natural state.

"I can take you out to where the barn once stood, however. That should give you a feel for the movements that Stella and her killer took on the day she died."

I nodded, took one last look at the wooded path, and then followed Cass to his car. We had to take the long way around, but when he reached the spot on Aspen Drive where the wooded trail came out, he stopped and pointed it out.

"There is nothing but forest for as far as you can see in any direction," I said.

Cass nodded.

"I can totally see the killer sitting here, waiting for someone to emerge from that little path. My question is, was the killer waiting for Stella specifically, or was she just in the wrong place at the wrong time?"

"The deputy didn't know. The path is not widely used, but as it turns out, there were a few students who took this route to get to this neighborhood, especially the ones who lived at this end of it."

"So it is feasible that the killer was waiting to nab whoever appeared first and that person just happened to be Stella?"

"Yes. That is not only feasible but likely. Keep in mind that on any other day, Stella would have been walking with you, and as you've already pointed out, the two of you tended to stick to the road."

There it was again. The guilt. The knowledge that if not for me and the fight I'd most likely picked, Stella would still be alive today.

Cass pulled back onto the road and continued on toward the land where the barn where Stella was most likely killed had once stood.

"I remember hearing that it was determined that Stella wasn't sexually assaulted. Was that true? I often wondered if that fact wasn't a rumor started to protect her and her family."

"According to the medical examiner's report, Stella was not sexually assaulted. Keep in mind that her body was partially decayed, so determining all the specifics was difficult, but from what I read, Stella was most likely strangled and then clawed with something capable of inflicting marks on the bone. It was never determined with any certainty if she was strangled or clawed first, but the ME suspected the claw marks were inflicted after she was already dead."

"Why would anyone do that? I get that there are psychos out there who strangle people, but what is up with the claw marks?"

Cass parked the car, opened his door, and got out. "I wish I knew."

I followed his lead and got out as well. I stood near the car and looked around. The parcel where the barn had once stood was hidden in the trees and sheltered from the road. I supposed that if someone wanted a quiet place to kill someone, this was as good a place as any.

"After Stella died, she was driven around the lake and buried in the woods. I wonder why. There are plenty of woods around here to hide a body. Why take the risk of transporting your kill around the lake if you didn't have to?"

"I'm not sure if the burial site had meaning to the killer or if he randomly picked an isolated location to bury his prey."

I hated that Cass referred to Stella as prey, but that's what she had been. To him. To the animal who'd killed her.

"And Tracy?" I asked. "We know she was last seen at the middle school and that she ended up buried a few yards from where Stella's body was found. Do you think he might have brought her here to kill her or somewhere nearby?"

"Perhaps. I've searched all the vacant barns in the area. There are only two." Cass put his hands on his hips and scanned the area. "There are a lot of woods out there. If the killer found another location, such as a cave or drainpipe to conceal his deeds, he could have taken her anywhere."

"What about Milo?" I looked back toward the vehicle. "Where is Milo anyway?"

"He is home today. When I woke up, he seemed to be feeling off, and I was only planning on doing follow-up calls, so I left him home to rest." Cass looked at his watch. "I should stop by the house to check on him after we leave here."

I suddenly realized I hadn't been to Cass's house since I'd been home. I'd enjoy seeing where he lived. "Should we head around the lake to the gravesite?" I asked. "Just to close the loop?"

"That works for me. I live over in that direction anyway."

As it turned out, Cass lived in a converted boathouse right on the lake. I should have known he'd choose somewhere he would be able to literally fish from his front door.

"Wow. This is really great. And it is so you."

"It's small, but Milo and I love it."

"I would think so." I stood on the dock, which linked the drive and the forest with the front door to the boathouse. I could totally picture Cass sitting out here on the porch swing, which sat on a dock that literally covered the water. "Can I see the inside?"

"Sure. If you don't mind a bit of a mess."

When Cass opened the door, Milo came bounding out. He looked fine to me. I wondered about the funky behavior Cass had described until we walked in the front door and found a pile of dog puke.

"It looks like he ate a tree."

Cass laughed. "Not a tree, but the silly dog does have a habit of eating sticks if I'm not watching him every minute." Cass headed to the kitchen for paper towels and floor cleaner. At least the floor was wood and not carpet. It should clean right up.

"Well, at least he seems to be feeling better," I said.

"He usually does once he gets whatever he's eaten out of his system." Cass bent down to clean up the mess. "I'll take him with us when we go. Now that he's feeling better, he won't want to stay home."

"Are you worried he'll eat the wrong thing and really make himself sick?" I asked.

"I am. But he is a dog, and I let him run around the property when I'm home. I can't watch him every minute of every day. I hoped he'd grow out of it at some point, but so far, he hasn't. Remember that lab I had when we were kids?"

"Sure."

"He liked grass. We struggled through an ongoing cycle of him eating grass and then puking it up from the day I brought him home until the day he died. I tried to train it out of him, but that dog liked grass. Short of keeping him indoors or on a leash at all times, there was no way I was going to keep him from eating it."

"Yeah, I get that." I looked around. "There is grass everywhere. Except in winter."

"Winter and snow gave us both a break."

I stepped farther into the room. Cass had a small living area that looked out at the lake, an even smaller kitchen, a bath off the kitchen, and a loft where he slept. In a way, his home reminded me of Naomi's cabin, only this was even smaller than hers, and of course, this was literally right on the water.

"I'll grab Milo's vest and leash, and then we can continue on to the burial sites."

"Okay. I'm going to take another look outside."

The location Stella's killer had chosen to bury her was only about five minutes from Cass's boathouse. The grave had eventually been found in a wooded area behind the campground. Stella had gone missing in the fall after the campground had closed for the season. As far as burial sites went, the killer hadn't chosen a bad one. This entire end of the lake was pretty deserted from mid-September through mid-May.

"And Tracy was found near here?" I asked Cass after he led me to Stella's temporary gravesite.

"Yeah. Just over here." He led the way.

"And Patricia?"

"Closer to the water." He walked in the direction of the lake. There was still yellow tape sectioning off the location where Patricia's remains had been found.

"In terms of location, Patricia could have been buried by the same person who buried Stella and Tracy."

"Yes, but everyone knew where Tracy's body was found. It was in the newspaper and all over town. I don't think the same person killed both girls. I can't prove it yet, but I will."

"When Stella was found, that was in the news as well," I pointed out.

"Yeah, I guess it was."

"So theoretically, the person who buried Tracy could have been someone other than the one who buried Stella, but knew about it and decided to bury Tracy here as well."

"Theoretically, yes. But that isn't what I think happened."

I took several steps toward the water and looked at my reflection. "Yeah. Me neither." I picked up a rock and tossed it, causing ripples on the surface. "So, what now? Does anything we've done today help you figure out who killed those girls?"

Cass frowned. Milo trotted over and sat at his feet as if sensing that his best buddy needed his support. "I have this gut feeling that there is something staring me in the face that I'm just not homing in on. We don't have a lot to go on in terms of Stella and Tracy's murders, but I do have a lot of leads to follow up on in regard to Patricia's death, so I'll start there. If I can find her killer and prove that person didn't kill Tracy, at least I'll have that to work from."

"Have you eliminated any of the suspects you told me about?"

"Actually, I have. I spoke to Walter Young, who has an alibi and was nowhere near the party when Patricia went missing, and I spoke to a friend of Patricia's who swears she was with Gayleen at the party and that they eventually left together. Unless she is lying, and I have no reason to believe she is, Gayleen didn't have the opportunity to kill and bury Patricia."

"So that just leaves the boyfriend and the teacher who should never have been at the party in the first place."

"As well as a few others whose names have come up. I have several interviews lined up for later this afternoon, so I hope I'll know more by the end of the day."

Cass called Milo and headed toward the car.

"Will you be at the shelter this afternoon?"

"I'm not sure," he answered. "Probably not if I am making progress in the case."

"I'll be working in the ticket booth at the haunted barn this evening. Maybe if you don't make it to the shelter, you can meet me there. We can grab a bite after."

Cass turned and looked at me. He smiled. "I'd like that."

CHAPTER 21

"I guess I was expecting a decent turnout, but there was no way I was expecting this," I said to Naomi, who just happened to have a volunteer shift at the haunted barn that paralleled my own.

"The haunted barn is always a popular event. We have a good turnout every year, especially on opening night. Most folks want a chance to go through before everyone posts about their experience on social media and spoils the surprises along the way."

"I get that. It does seem like if you tape a show or are planning to attend an event on any night other than the first, you'd better stay off social media if you are worried about spoilers." I looked out at the line that wound around the parking lot. "I don't see how they are going to get all these people thorough before the barn closes at midnight."

"Not our problem because our shift ends at ten."

"I guess." I had to admit to having my doubts that we'd get out of here on time. I hoped so because I hadn't eaten and I was starving. Maybe making plans with Cass had been a bad idea. "I just hope our relief shows up by ten. I'm both starving and exhausted."

"You did really well with the training today. Did it feel a bit more natural than it did on Tuesday?"

"It did, yes. I had a much better idea of what to do and how to relate to the dogs I worked with. I'm looking forward to my shifts next week, and of course, volunteering with Cass is a blast. I missed him this afternoon."

"I guess he had to work."

I nodded. "He has two murder cases to solve, both of which are pretty complex."

"Are you still thinking that Stella and Tracy's deaths are linked, but Patricia's isn't?"

I nodded as I counted out the change due to the person I'd been helping. I wasn't sure we should be talking about this here in the ticket booth of one of the busiest events of the entire year, but no one seemed to be paying any attention to us, and we were standing in a secure building with a glass enclosure between us and the customers we were serving. "Cass and I retraced Stella's final afternoon this morning. We started at the middle school, then went to the site where the barn where it is believed she died used to be, and then on to the burial site. I have to say the entire experience was very sobering."

"Did you learn anything?"

"I don't know that Cass learned anything he didn't already know, but I found out for the first time that Stella hadn't taken the normal route the two of us usually did that day."

"She didn't?"

"She took the wooded path that starts behind the baseball field and ends up on Aspen Drive. Cass thinks that someone might have been waiting in a car on Aspen Drive for school to get out, and Stella just happened to be in the wrong place at the wrong time."

Naomi frowned. "I know the exact place you are talking about. I know we weren't close in middle school, so you might not know that I was on the track team."

"I sort of remember you were on the track team in high school."

"Middle school too. I used to run a loop that took me north from the middle school through the woods, across Aspen Drive, north of the place you are talking about, then south through the woods, and then I'd cross the very spot you are describing, and end up back at the school."

"Did you see anything on the day Stella went missing?"

She shrugged. "Not that I remember. But I did see an old truck parked on the road near the little footpath that connected Aspen Drive with the school on numerous occasions that fall."

I paused and gave Naomi my full attention. "Did you see anyone in the truck?"

She shook her head and then continued to count out change and sell tickets. "No. Not that I can remember. The truck was old and beat up. I don't remember seeing anyone in the cab, but there was a camper on the back. I guess someone could have been inside that."

"Did you ever see anyone lurking around nearby?"

"There was this one time when I saw a man partially hidden in the dense forest off to the side. It looked like he was going to approach me, so I picked up my pace and took off as fast as I could. After that, whenever I saw the truck on the road, I took the long way around to get back to the school."

"Did you tell the deputy who was looking into Stella's murder about that truck?" I asked as I handed a woman the ten tickets she'd asked for.

"No. He never asked, and to be honest, I didn't make the connection until just now. I'd seen you and Stella walking along the road after school a bunch of times when I was out running. I assumed she was abducted somewhere along the main route to her house."

"We should tell Cass what you just remembered," I said. I looked out at the ticket line, which seemed to have just gotten longer. "I need to take a quick break to call him. Will you be okay?"

"Yeah. I'll be fine. Tell him the truck was white with a lot of dents and rust, and the camper was sort of a brown and tan color, also old. I doubt the truck is still around. It looked to be on its last legs twenty years ago, but I suppose you never know."

I could hear the complaints from the line when I closed my window and announced that I was going on a short break. The ticket booth was a portable shed of sorts with windows that opened and closed and an interior counter that the service organizations in the area had purchased to use for this purpose. In addition to being useful, it could be locked up, which meant it was secure.

"Hey, Cass, it's Callie," I said after I stepped away to make my call.

"I was just about to head in your direction."

"That's great, but I have something to tell you that I don't think can wait. Naomi just told me that she ran track in middle school, and during the weeks before Stella went missing she saw an old truck with a camper parked on Aspen Drive right near the trail leading back to the school."

"An old truck with a camper. A white truck with a brown camper?"

"Yeah. So you knew about it."

"No. Not in connection with Stella at least. But someone I spoke to when Tracy went missing mentioned an old white truck with a brown camper that had been seen parked on the road near the middle school."

"It can't be the same truck. Naomi said the one she saw was old twenty years ago."

"It might be unlikely that it is the same truck, but it is possible. I'm heading out now. Tell Naomi I'll want to talk to her. Tell her not to leave until I get there."

I hung up, returned to the ticket booth, and reopened my window. I passed on Cass's message to Naomi and then got busy selling tickets. It looked as if the line was somewhat shorter. I still didn't see how everyone was going to get through the haunted barn by midnight, but as Naomi had said, that wasn't our problem. Our replacements showed up right about the same time Cass did, so we turned things over to them, and the three of us headed back toward town, where Cass knew of an all-night diner.

It didn't take Cass and Naomi long to figure out that the truck she'd seen twenty years ago and the truck witnesses had seen near the middle school in the weeks before Tracy went missing were one and the same. Now, all Cass had to do was track it down. No one Cass had talked to had mentioned a license plate number, but he planned to go back to talk to everyone again. Maybe he'd be able to jog someone's memory. Even without the license number, Cass had enough to put out an APB on the truck. Given its age and the fact that it was a white truck with a brown camper, it didn't seem as if it would be too hard to find.

"I wonder if the same truck was seen in Rivers Bend before Hillary went missing," I said after we'd ordered and our coffee had been set down on our table.

"I'll pull the files and check," Cass answered.

"I feel like this is a real lead," I said, more confident that we'd find Stella's killer than I had been at any point before.

"Didn't anyone mention the truck when Stella went missing?" Naomi asked. "I mean sure, the stretch of road where it was parked is sparsely used, but it *is* used on occasion. Someone must have seen the truck parked there on the side of the road."

"I'll go back through everything again, but I don't remember seeing any mention of a truck in the original paperwork. Maybe, like you, anyone who saw the truck didn't think it being parked there was all that important."

"I guess. But it still seems like someone would have said something. I realize that I have no room to make a comment about others not mentioning the truck because I didn't either, but I was twelve, and no one asked me if I'd noticed any strange cars or trucks around, so it never occurred to me to bring it up."

"You told Callie you saw a man in the woods watching you on one occasion. Can you describe him?"

Naomi slowly shook her head. "It was so long ago, and I only got a glimpse of him. I wondered what he was doing just standing there behind the shrubs. But I can't remember much at all about him."

"Height? Weight?" Cass asked.

"Average, I guess. I know that doesn't help, but I don't remember that he stood out as being tall or short or thin or fat, so average is all I can come up with." She frowned. "He had a coat on." She furrowed her brows even deeper. "I remember that it was cool but not cold that day, and I thought it was strange that he had on such a long coat when it wasn't even snowing."

"Did you notice anything else?" Cass asked. "Was he holding anything?"

She shrugged. "I don't think so. It all happened really fast. I was jogging by, I noticed him standing there, and he took a step forward, which scared me, so I ran."

"And did you tell anyone that you'd seen the man when you got back to the school?"

Naomi's eyes widened. "I did mention it to someone. A man standing by the gym. I think he was a teacher, but I'm not sure. He might have been a parent. I told him there was a strange man lurking around in the woods and he told me he'd check it out."

"And then?" Cass asked.

"And then I headed to the locker room to shower."

"Was anyone else around besides the man you spoke to?"

"There was someone in the gym when I went through." She paused and tugged a bit more at the memory. "The volleyball team. I remember the girls were practicing."

"Stella was on the volleyball team," I said.

"So maybe the guy in the forest was there to watch the girls," Cass said. "How long before Stella went missing did this happen?"

"A while. Maybe a month. A few weeks at least."

"And after that day in the woods, did you ever see the man in the forest again?"

"No. Like I told you earlier, I changed my route and started sticking to the main roads after the man scared me."

CHAPTER 22

Saturday

As tired as I was, sleep evaded me. After hours of tossing and turning and getting nowhere, I finally got up and went up to the attic. There was a voice in the back of my mind that seemed to be nagging at me with the idea that perhaps the secret to finding Stella's killer, and Tracy's as well, was in some random piece of information I had at my disposal. Could my twelve-year-old self have known something I didn't even realize? Apparently, Naomi's twelve-year-old self had known something that might very well identify who'd killed Stella after all these years.

"Where do I even start?" I asked Alastair.

"Meow." He trotted across the room and pawed at the box where I'd found the journal I'd kept after Stella died.

I bent down to take a look. In addition to old books, I found photo albums, old notebooks, and even the Nancy Drew log Stella and I kept during our girl detective phase. We'd outgrown that before entering middle school, so I didn't think there would be clues inside the log, though we had kept it well into the summer after sixth grade, and Stella had died in the fall of seventh grade, so maybe there could be.

"'April 12th,'" I read aloud. "'*The Case of the Missing Homework.*'" I smiled. Most of our cases were pretty silly, but Stella and I'd had a lot of fun pretending to be girl detectives. I continued to read. "'Stella is sure she did her English homework this week, which required us to do a biography with photos from our life. When she went to hand it in, the homework she is sure she put in her backpack that morning was missing. Mrs. Brubaker is threatening detention unless she redoes the paper by the end of the week.'"

I looked at Alastair. "I remember this. Stella was so mad."

"Meow."

"'After examining the facts, we decided that someone had taken it from her backpack after we arrived at school but before the first bell rang.'"

"Meow."

"Yeah, it would be an odd item for someone to steal, but it was possible because we'd leave our backpacks next to the door of our classroom and then head to the playground to hang out on the monkey bars. Still, who would steal an assignment like that? It wasn't like Stella was missing some generic math homework that someone who didn't do the assignment could copy and turn in as their own." I mulled the thought in my mind a bit more. "I sort of remember that Stella found other stuff missing from her backpack. A brush. Lip gloss. I think even a half-eaten apple."

"Meow."

"If Stella had a stalker, that would explain a lot." I thought about the old truck parked near the school. I thought about the man Naomi had seen in the woods twenty years ago, and the man who'd been hanging out in the field behind the school when Tracy disappeared. Was it possible they were the same person?

It was too early to call Cass, so I texted him. I figured he could call me when he got up. In the meantime, I continued on to the photo album. I was pretty sure I had photos of Stella and me in the weeks leading up to her death.

Most of the photos had been taken at my house or hers, but there were a few taken in town and even a series taken at the middle school during our first week of classes. I remembered how excited we were to finally leave our childhood behind when we'd become mature and sophisticated middle school students. We'd felt so grown-up. High school was just around the corner, and Stella and I had definite plans to rock our teenage years before moving on to college. But Stella had died, and I'd become even more introverted than I already was, so none of the dreams we'd shared during those first few weeks of seventh grade ever came true.

I paused at a photo I'd taken of Stella in her volleyball uniform. She stood with the ball resting against her hip as she prepared to attend her first practice. The smile of innocence on her face sent sheer pain through my heart. I ran a finger over her form. "I'm so very sorry."

I was about to turn the page when I noticed a truck parked on the street that paralleled the school, which was clearly visible in the background. White truck, brown camper.

CHAPTER 23

Cass called shortly after I'd jumped in the shower to get ready for my shift volunteering at the Harvest Festival. He left a message on my voice mail, letting me know he was heading out to follow up on a lead in Patricia Long's death and would call me when he returned to the office. I didn't figure there was a lot I could do in the meantime, so I dressed in layers and headed to the park in the center of town.

"You've been assigned to the ring toss," Hope informed me. "Anyone who wants to try their skill will give you a ticket they will have already purchased, and you will give them five rings." She handed me a sheet of paper. "Here is the key to show you which prize to give them. One ring on a bottle is a small prize, two a slightly larger prize, and so on."

"Looks self-explanatory," I said.

"It's one of the easier games to monitor. Just be sure that everyone gets into a single line and that only one person is given rings to toss at a time. If you have questions, you can ask one of the other volunteers. Most of the locals volunteer every year and know exactly what to do."

"Okay, thanks." I took the rings and the jar into which I was to deposit the tickets I collected and headed toward my booth. The place was already busy. The volunteers had all come early and most had brought family members who were wandering around, waiting for the games to start.

By the time Hope's voice came over the loudspeaker announcing that the games had officially opened, long lines had already formed at each game. I stepped up to the railing with my rings and greeted the first person in line. I took his ticket, handed him the five rings, and then waited while he tossed them. Two of the five landed around a bottle's neck, so I handed him the appropriate prize, gathered the rings, and greeted the next person in line.

Things continued to run like clockwork for the first half hour until Billy wandered into my line.

"I'm sorry, but you'll need to go to the end of the line," I said when he pushed his way to the front.

"I was in line. You just didn't see me."

"No," I countered. "You were not in line. I saw you come over from the game across from us and squeeze into the front. As I said, if you want to play this game, you will need to go to the end of the line."

"Make me."

Oh, how I wanted to. How I wanted to leap over the barrier in front of me, take the smart mouthed tween by the shoulders, and forcefully set him to the side. Of course, I'd probably get arrested for assaulting a minor, and he'd get off scot-free.

"Come on, Billy, let's go to another booth," his friend said.

I sent the friend a smile of gratitude, which seemed to make Billy dig in his heels even deeper. He held out his hand. "The rings, lady."

I wanted to say "bite me," but instead, I simply crossed my arms over my chest. I looked at the long line behind Billy. If I just let him play, he'd move on, and then the line could move up, but there was no way I was letting this punk get the better of me. "If you don't go to the end of the line, I'll have to close the booth, and then no one will get to play."

That got Billy's peers grumbling. I waited for someone from the line—someone Billy's age and therefore unlikely to get arrested for child abuse—to take matters into their own hands and move the obnoxious child along.

Surprisingly, no one did as I'd expected. Maybe Billy was one of those kids everyone was afraid of.

"Is there a problem here?" a man who looked vaguely familiar, though I couldn't place him, stepped up to the front of the line.

"I'm afraid this young man has cut the line and is holding up everything," I answered, figuring the man, who looked to be about forty, was one of the parents.

"Let's move along, shall we?" he said to Billy.

Billy nodded and walked away. I was about to thank the man when he walked away as well. It was then I noticed the prosthetic hand.

Oh my God, I thought to myself. The man I was more and more sure had killed two children was here at the festival, where there were hundreds of children to prey on.

"I need to take a break," I announced to the line. I jumped over the barrier, creating a chorus of protests, and then followed the man toward the parking area. When I saw him climb into an old pickup—white truck, brown camper—I knew that the man we first suspected of killing Tracy was the one who actually had.

"Pick up, pick up," I said after dialing Cass's cell.

"Hey, Callie. I'm kind of busy; can I call you back?"

"The man who has been hanging around the middle school is here. Or at least he was."

"Here where?"

"The Harvest Festival, where I am supposed to be volunteering."

"I see. Is there a problem?"

"I found a photo in Gracie's attic. The same man was at the middle school when Stella died. He has to be the killer."

"Both Stella and Tracy were strangled, and Craig Grainger has a prosthetic hand. There is no way he strangled anyone."

"I know about the hand, but the guy just left here in a truck. A white truck with a brown camper."

Cass paused. "Okay. I need to finish up here, then I'll come to meet you. Give me thirty minutes. Meet me by the snack bar."

Thirty minutes might not seem like a lot of time in the grand scheme of things, but when you were certain that you'd just seen a serial killer drive away, it seemed like an eternity.

I used the time to find Hope to let her know that I'd had to abandon the game. I headed back into the festival crowd. I was pretty sure Hope would be at the entrance, where a volunteers' check-in table was set up, so I went in that direction. When I arrived, I pulled her aside to fill her in on the situation. She assured me that meeting with Cass was a lot more important if doing so would help him find Tracy's killer, and that she'd find someone else to cover the ring toss.

By the time I'd explained things to Hope, Cass had arrived, and I followed him out toward the parking area, where I'd last seen the white truck with the brown camper.

"Okay, exactly what happened?" Cass asked.

"I was working the ring toss when this brat cut the line. I told him to go to the end of the line, but he wouldn't. We ended up in a battle of wills that seemed as if it was never going to find a resolution when a man walked up. He asked what the problem was, and thinking he was another volunteer or a parent, I explained, he told the kid to move on, and he did just as he was asked. I was going to thank the guy for helping me out, but he walked away too quickly. It was then I noticed he had a prosthetic hand. I followed him out to the parking lot and saw him get into an old white truck with a brown camper." I took a breath. "And there's more. I was looking through some old photo albums I'd left up in Gracie's attic this morning and found one from when Stella and I had just started middle school. I took a photo of her on her first day of volleyball practice, and the truck I saw this man get into was in the background. I am sure that was the same man Naomi described for us, the man she'd seen in the woods, and I suspect he is the same man Anna told Paisley about."

Cass blew out a breath. "Okay. I still don't see how Craig Grainger could have done what was done to Stella and Tracy with only one hand, but I'll talk to him again."

"Can I come with you?"

He hesitated.

"Please. I'll stay out of the way."

"You can ride along, but only if you agree to wait in the car."

I'd hoped that Cass would let me listen in on their conversation, but waiting in the car was better than nothing, so I agreed to his terms. He suggested that I leave my car at the festival and come back for it later. I supposed I should call both Gracie and Paisley to let them know I might not make it to the pumpkin patch as we'd planned, although I hated to disappoint Paisley. I decided to see how Cass's interview went and take it from there.

CHAPTER 24

"So you are telling me that this man with the truck was seen lurking around the middle school twenty years ago when Stella disappeared and then again recently when Tracy went missing, but Cass is sure that he is not the killer?" Gracie asked later in the day as we walked around the pumpkin patch. Paisley was walking ahead of us with Tom, who was pulling a wagon to carry the pumpkins she picked out.

"That's what he said. He spoke to the man, who admitted that he likes to watch kids. That in and of itself seems creepy to me, but Cass said there is absolutely nothing to suggest that the man has ever harmed any of the kids he watches sexually or otherwise, and a perusal of the police reports surrounding Hillary's death in Rivers Bend did not mention a white truck with a brown camper or a creepy man hanging around the school."

"Can't Cass arrest him for hanging around the school? It doesn't seem right."

"He can't arrest him because he hasn't actually done anything wrong, but Cass talked to him again today about finding another place to hang out. According to Cass, the man was in a car accident when he was in middle school. I guess he was pretty banged up and not only did he lose a hand, but he suffered injury to his brain as well. Cass seems to think the man's fascination with kids in this age group is due to that brain injury. He is going to keep an eye on him and is going to keep strongly encouraging him to hang out somewhere else, but not a single student that Cass has talked to has reported any wrongdoing on the man's part. He hangs back and watches, and some of the kids go over to talk to him, but that seems to be the extent of it."

"I take it he doesn't work?"

"Cass said he is on disability."

"And when Naomi saw him in the woods?" Gracie asked.

"Cass suspects the guy was just lurking then too and didn't mean to scare her or mean her any harm."

"I still don't like it."

"None of us do. Still, it really doesn't look like the guy is the killer, so Cass is basically back to square one. At least with Stella and Tracy's cases. He said he is making progress with Patricia Long's death, but he declined to fill me in at this point."

"How about this one?" Paisley held up a large pumpkin.

"I like it," I called back. "It's round and big enough to carve. Now we just need to find three more like it."

"I see one over there." Paisley put the pumpkin in the wagon and took off running.

I couldn't help but smile. It had been a long time since I'd felt that much enthusiasm for anything, but there had been a time when I too could barely contain my happiness. As I watched Paisley run from one pumpkin to another, I had to wonder what had happened to that girl. I guess there comes a time when we leave the wonder of childhood behind, only to replace it with the responsibility of adulthood, but what I wouldn't give to feel that happy again if only for a day.

"Should we carve them when we get home?" Paisley asked when the wagon was full.

"I think that would be a wonderful idea," I said. I looked at Aunt Gracie. "As long as it is okay with you."

"Fine by me. I'll heat up the chili and make some corn bread, and we can carve straight through the dinner hour."

"Be sure to call your grandmother to let her know what we are doing," I counseled. "We wouldn't want her to worry."

"I'll call her. She won't worry as long as I am with you and I have a ride home."

"I can drive you home when we're done," I offered.

During the next few hours, I remembered what it was like to be a kid again. I remembered what it was like to find pure joy in the simple things. I remembered what it was like to laugh without inhibition. I remembered the magic I'd somehow lost along the way. There would be those who would say my friendship with Paisley had been beneficial to her, and I hoped that was true. But the truth of the matter was our friendship was helping me more than I could ever say.

"Cass just pulled up," Gracie called out to me just as I was getting ready to take Paisley home.

I hesitated.

"I'll take her," Gracie offered. "There is leftover chili in the refrigerator if Cass is hungry."

"Thanks, Aunt Gracie." I hugged Paisley. "I'll see you tomorrow for your piano lesson."

"I'll be here." She hugged me back.

Cass came in through the back door just as Gracie and Paisley were leaving. Tom went with them as well.

"Hungry?" I asked.

"Starving."

"There is leftover chili and corn bread."

"Sounds perfect."

I grabbed a beer and popped the top before passing it to Cass. "So, how'd it go?" I asked. "Did your lead pay off?"

"It did."

"And?"

"And Patricia's killer is behind bars."

I frowned as I sliced the corn bread. "That seems like it would be a good thing, but you don't seem happy."

He ran a hand through his hair. "I'm not. The case was a rough one."

I scooped the chili into a bowl and put it in the microwave. "Do you want to talk about it?"

"It isn't pretty," he warned.

I set the plate with the corn bread and honey butter on the table. "I'm a big girl. I'm sure I can take whatever it is."

Cass took a sip of his beer. "It turns out that Patricia had an older step brother who lived with the family."

Oh, God. I already hated where this was going.

"The brother, who just turned twenty, had been molesting her for years. Patricia never told a soul until recently, when, after a few beers they'd snuck from her dad's stash, she'd come clean with a friend. The friend persuaded her to tell her mom, which she planned to do as soon as her mom returned from visiting her aunt. Somehow, the brother found out. When she arrived home early from the party after arguing with her boyfriend, the brother just happened to be the only one at home. He confronted her, she fought back, and he killed her."

"Oh, God."

Cass continued. "He'd read the details of Tracy's death in the newspaper and decided to make it look like the person who killed Tracy also killed Patricia."

"The scratch marks?"

"He scratched her with his nails after she was dead, which, as it turns out, was a good thing, because we found skin under his nails that we will use to send the guy to prison for a very long time."

"So who put you on to the brother?" I wondered.

"The friend Patricia told her secret to. After Patricia turned up dead, she wondered if it hadn't been the brother. It took her a few days to work up the courage to tell me what she knew, but eventually, she did the right thing."

"I hate that Patricia was killed by a family member."

"Yeah." Cass sighed. "Me too. He wasn't blood, but still. It was not the sort of ending anyone wants to see."

I poured myself a glass of wine and sat down across from Cass. "So it looks like Patricia's death is definitely not linked to Tracy's."

"I guess not."

"Where does that leave Buck? I mean, the whole reason the sheriff released him was because Buck couldn't have killed Patricia. Now that you know the two deaths were not carried out by the same person, will you rearrest him for Tracy's murder?"

Cass frowned. "I still don't think that Buck killed Tracy, but I do think he might be able to help us figure out who did."

"How is that?"

"It seemed as if Buck was covering for someone. I'm not sure if he was being bribed or threatened to do so, but if we find out who Buck was protecting, it seems like we should be able to identify the killer."

CHAPTER 25

Sunday

Once again, I found myself sitting in the attic with Alastair in the wee hours of the morning. I'd tried to go back to sleep after waking when a noise outside my bedroom window startled me, but as hard as I tried, sleep evaded me. I wasn't sure why I spent so much time up here. I guess it was the one place in all the world I felt the safest. I'd spent most of my time up here when I came to live with Gracie after my parents died, and I'd almost lived up here after Stella was murdered and any innocence I might still have possessed had been completely destroyed.

I plucked the Nancy Drew journal Stella and I had kept off the pile of books where I'd left it and curled into the window to read. Most of the cases Stella and I took on were silly. I opened the book to find a page entitled *The Case of the Missing Sock*, which was followed by *The Case of the Too-Salty Casserole*. That one was a toughie. It seemed that the casserole Stella's mom had made for dinner turned out too salty and she blamed the grandmother, who'd been visiting at the time, saying that she'd added salt to it after she'd finished mixing it and transferred it to the casserole dish for baking. The grandmother denied having done so, and an argument erupted between the two, which for some reason, Stella thought she could mediate by finding the truth about the too-salty casserole.

I smiled as I remembered the fun Stella and I'd had. I don't think we ever did figure out how the casserole came to be too salty, but we did find that missing sock. The cases we opened became spaced further and further apart as we got ready to enter middle school. I think we both decided somewhere along the way that participating in a Nancy Drew club was for babies.

I opened the book to the end in an attempt to remember our last case. *The Case of the Peeping Tom.* I frowned. I'd totally forgotten about this one, which had been opened by Stella shortly after we started middle school. She was sure that someone was spying on her. I remember that she thought someone had been looking through the air vent in the girls' locker room while she was changing for volleyball. How could I have forgotten about this? Sure, I'd been traumatized beyond description when Stella was murdered, and I pretty much blocked everything from my mind. But this? Why hadn't I realized that a Peeping Tom would be an important thing to know about when investigating a murder?

I looked at the notes.

Day 1 – *Someone was watching me through the vent in the girls' locker room.* The notation was written in Stella's handwriting. *I could hear someone breathing, but I couldn't see their face.*

Day 2 was written in my handwriting. *I spoke to the other girls on the volleyball team. Several of the others reported a similar experience to the one Stella reported.*

Day 3 was recorded by Stella. *Chills were experienced when the creepy art sub watched me walk away after class. I think I might fake being sick tomorrow.*

Art sub? I didn't take art because I had private piano lessons during sixth period, which counted as my elective. I wondered if we could find out who the sub for Stella's art class had been. I made a mental note to ask Cass. It was twenty years ago, but it would seem that employee records were kept forever.

Day 4 was again recorded by me. *This case is closed on account of Stella being a big baby I am never going to speak to again.*

Oh, God. I must have written that on the day Stella went missing. I guess that would explain why we'd never closed the case as we usually did. I guess it also explained why the logbook was left in my possession. I'd been the one to have it when Stella had died.

It was too early to call Cass, so I texted him and told him I had an important piece of news and that he should call me as soon as he woke up. A sub. Of course. We suspected the killer might be a substitute for the county. In my gut, I knew that if we could identify the person who subbed for Stella's art class, we would find the killer.

Of course, once I'd stumbled upon this piece of information, I became hugely impatient. Cass was a deputy. He was probably used to being woken up in the middle of the night. Surely, he wouldn't mind if I called his cell even though it was only four fifteen in the morning.

I called. He didn't answer.

Dang. Maybe I should try 911, but this really wasn't an emergency. Making a quick decision, I jogged downstairs to my room, pulled on some clothes, and headed out into the night. If Goliath wasn't going to answer the phone, the mountain was going to go to Goliath. Or something like that.

When I arrived at Cass's, I found his vehicle gone. I knocked on the door, and he didn't answer. Milo came to the door barking like he was going to kill whoever was on the other side. I waited to see if the barking would wake Cass, but when he still didn't come to the door, I figured he was out. But where could he be? It was still a couple of hours until sunrise.

I returned to my car and considered what to do next. I supposed Cass might have been called out on a call. Patricia's murder had been wrapped up, so he could have responded to a call connected to Tracy's murder, or he might be out on a call of a different sort altogether. Should I wait? Head home? Drive into town and go by the station to see if he was there?

I tried calling his cell again, but the call went directly to voice mail. I had to admit this had me worried. Despite the voice in my head telling me to wait before acting, I found myself calling Naomi, who answered right away.

"Callie? Is everything okay?"

"I'm looking for Cass. I have this gut feeling he might be in trouble, and I need your help."

"Of course. What can I do?"

"The story you told us about running through the woods and seeing the man in the coat and then telling an adult who was watching the girls practice volleyball. Can you remember what the man looked like?"

"The man in the woods?"

"No, the man watching the game. The one you told about the man in the woods."

"Wow. I don't know. It's been so long."

"Try to remember what you can. It might be important."

"Okay." She paused. "I remember he looked familiar, yet I didn't know his name. I think he had dark hair. Short. I don't know. I didn't pay all that much attention."

"Stella thought the man who was subbing for the art class was watching her. Do you remember him?"

"I had marching band, so I didn't have art."

I tried to remember what Cass had told me about Harvey Underwood's schedule at the middle school the year that Stella died. "I think the same guy subbed for Mr. Donnelly's history class later in the year."

"Oh, wait. I know who you are talking about." She paused. I supposed she must have been thinking about what she'd seen, attempting to remember.

Eventually, she spoke. "Yeah, now that you say that, I do think it might have been him. The thing with the guy in the forest happened early in the school year and the guy you are talking about who took over Donnelly's class when his wife had a baby, subbed for him late in the year. I'd never made the connection, but it totally might have been him."

"His name was Mr. Underwood. Does that ring a bell?"

"Not really. It was twenty years ago," she reminded me.

"I know. But I suspect that Underwood might be the killer Cass is looking for. He worked as a sub here in Foxtail Lake when both Stella and Tracy died, and he worked in Rivers Bend when Hillary died."

"Hillary?"

I explained who she was and how her death compared to Stella and Tracy's.

"Does Cass know this?" Naomi asked.

"He does. He was at my place last evening, and when he left, he told me he was going to track down Buck Darwin and attempt to find out who he was covering for. I didn't think he was going to do that last night, but I've tried calling him, and it went straight to voice mail. I'm at his place right now, and he isn't here. I'm worried that Darwin told him what he wanted to know, and he went after the killer alone only to have the killer turn the tables on him."

"And you think Mr. Underwood is the killer?"

"It fits. He was in all the right places at the right times. Stella thought he was watching her. You found him watching the girls' volleyball team of which Stella was a member on the day of your encounter in the woods."

"So what do we do?"

"I don't know. I guess we call one of the other deputies assigned to the town." I thought about the options.

"Rafe volunteers for me sometimes. I have his number. I'll call him. Why don't you come over here and we can figure this out together?"

"Okay. I'm on my way."

CHAPTER 26

The lights were bright, the air stale, and I felt like I couldn't breathe. I was sure I was going to be sick, but I suppressed the urge.

"Dr. Whilton you are needed in the OR," someone said over the loudspeaker.

"It's going to be okay." Naomi squeezed my hand.

"What is taking so long?" I asked for the tenth time in ten minutes.

"These things take time."

I supposed they did. God, I hated hospitals. I'd spent as much time in one as I ever wanted to, but I couldn't leave. Not with Cass in critical condition. "What if he doesn't make it?"

"He will."

"He lost a lot of blood."

"Which is why God invented transfusions. Try to relax. You look like you are going to pass out."

I glanced at Naomi and nodded. Passing out in an effort to escape the lights and the noise wasn't the worst idea. I remembered the lights, the noise, the smell of vomit and blood after my own accident. I thought I was going to die. I hadn't died as I thought I might, but there had been times during my recovery after the accident, before I came back to Foxtail Lake, that I'd wished I had.

"I wonder when Rafe will get here."

"I don't know. He said he'd be by when he had the chance. Here comes the doctor," Naomi said.

I stood up on wobbly legs. She stood up next to me, still clinging to my hand. I wanted to hear what the doctor had to say, but at the same time, I didn't. What if Cass was dead? What if the bullet that pierced his chest had ended his life?

"Deputy Wylander is out of surgery. It went well. He is still in critical yet stable condition, but barring further complications, I expect a full recovery."

"Can I see him?" I asked.

"He is still in the recovery room. He won't wake up for hours. I'm going to suggest the two of you go home. Get something to eat. I can call when he wakes up."

I wanted to say no. I wanted to inform the man that I'd stay right here until I could see he was fine with my own eyes, but Naomi responded to the doctor before I was able, agreeing to his suggestion. She led me out of the hospital into the bright sunshine. I squinted against the intensity.

"How about we do as the doctor suggested and get something to eat?" Naomi asked.

"Let's go to Gracie's. She'll be worried. I should check in with her, and I'm sure she'd happily make us something to eat."

"Okay. If you're sure."

"I am."

The ride to the lake house was accomplished in silence. After Naomi had gotten hold of Rafe and told him my story, he'd tracked down Underwood's address. When he arrived at his home, he'd found Underwood gone and Cass in a pool of blood on his front porch. He'd been shot in the chest and had lost a lot of blood by the time the ambulance arrived. I remembered the attendant saying that it would be a miracle if he made it to the hospital alive. Thankfully, in this instance, we'd gotten our miracle.

"How is Cass?" Gracie asked the moment we pulled up.

"He's out of surgery," I answered. "Stable according to the doctor, but still in recovery."

"And Underwood?"

"Rafe went after him," Naomi said.

"He's a good deputy. He'll get him," Gracie said as if to convince herself. "Can I get you girls some breakfast?"

"Breakfast would be great," Naomi answered.

Personally, I didn't think I could eat, but if I didn't, Gracie would worry, so maybe a few bites. When I entered the kitchen, I found Tom on the phone. I wasn't sure who he was speaking to, but he seemed to be asking about the status of Underwood and the case in general. Everything in my being prayed they'd catch the monster who had killed three little girls and almost killed Cass.

I excused myself and went into the bathroom, where I sobbed out all the tears I'd been holding at bay. I cried for Stella, and Hillary, and Tracy, and Cass. I cried for the loss of my own innocence and the hell the families of all the victims had gone through. When I returned to the kitchen, everyone was smiling.

"They got him," Tom announced. "The state police got that bastard, and now he can rot in jail as he should have been doing for the past twenty years."

I half-expected Gracie to admonish Tom for using the B word—she was very anti cussing—but in this instance, she must have felt it was warranted because she simply smiled and hugged him.

"Did he confess?"

"No, but they found a hand trowel in the trunk of his car. They are sure it is the one used to carve claw marks in Tracy's face."

"Why would anyone do that?" Naomi asked.

"Maybe so they didn't have to look at the face of the person they'd just killed and deal with the guilt I have to assume even a monster would feel," Gracie said.

Perhaps Gracie was right. It did seem like Underwood was obsessed with Stella. Maybe he was obsessed with all of them. Maybe he strangled them in a fit of rage and then disfigured them to hide his guilt even from himself.

CHAPTER 27

Thursday

"One more house and then we are going to go to dinner," I said to Paisley. Cass, Gracie, Tom, and I had taken her trick-or-treating. Based on the hundreds of kids out and about, it looked like the town had already recovered from the fear following Tracy's death, although it did seem as if most of the kids were with adults.

"Can we get pizza?" asked Paisley, who'd chosen to wear my old Inspector Gadget costume.

"Did Cass put you up to asking for pizza?" I asked as she smiled at him and he winked at her.

"I'll never tell." She giggled before running up the walkway to what was going to be our last stop before heading into town.

"I can't believe you would use a child that way," I teased, standing next to him as he took a break and sat down on the low wall separating the lawn from the sidewalk.

Cass threw up his hands, in an effort, I was sure, to convince me of his innocence. He was taking things slowly tonight and had spent half the evening on a park bench with Tom, waiting for Paisley, Gracie, and me to do the house-to-house thing in the neighborhood near the park, but it turned out the bullet had not pierced any vital organs, so once they'd given him a transfusion and stitched him up, he recovered fairly quickly.

"Actually, I'm just glad you feel good enough to care what you eat," I added, taking his arm and hugging it to my chest. Tom and Gracie had gone on ahead to speak to a friend who participated in the same bridge club they did, so it was just the two of us for the moment. "I don't think I've ever been as scared in my life as I was when Rafe called Naomi to inform us that you'd been shot."

"I get that you were scared, and I would have been too if you were the one to have been shot, but I'm fine. You don't need to worry about me. This isn't even the first time I've been shot in the line of duty."

"It isn't?"

He shook his head.

"I didn't need to know that."

"I'm a deputy. Things happen."

I supposed that was true, but still. At least, despite the fact that I'd almost lost Cass, things had seemed to work out all right. Cass had spoken to Buck, as he'd indicated he planned to do, and Buck finally admitted that Underwood had both threatened and bribed him to take the fall for him after he'd seen the killer burying Tracy's body. Buck shared that Underwood had promised him untold riches if he cooperated and a painful death if he didn't, and Buck, who had been living in the campground, was just broken enough to believe him and act accordingly. The execution of Cass's plan to confront Underwood had gone flawlessly in the beginning, but the dismount had been pretty shaky when it turned out that Underwood had a gun. At least the claw he'd used to mark the faces of his victims had been found in his trunk, ensuring that he'd never again see the outside of a prison cell.

"When do you have to go back to work?" I asked Cass.

"Not for a while. The county requires me to be fully cleared by my doctor before I can return to active duty, and my doctor is a cautious guy."

I waved to Paisley, who was trotting back toward us. "I'm glad your doctor is the cautious sort. You need to allow your body to heal before you jump back into the ring."

"I told you I was fine."

"Maybe. But I'm happy you will have the time you need. Do you have any plans for your time off?"

Cass looked into the clear and starry sky. "It's warmed back up after the cold spell we had, so I thought I'd go fishing. I figure if the weather cooperates, I have a few weeks left before the season comes to an end." Cass grinned at me. "I don't suppose you'd want to keep me company?"

"If by fishing you actually mean fishing, sure. If by fishing you mean something else, I think I'll pass."

"What else would I mean by fishing other than fishing?" Cass tried to appear innocent, but I knew that he knew exactly what I meant.

"I do have Paisley's piano lessons and my volunteer shifts at the shelter to work around, and I suppose I should think about getting a job of some sort."

"So you are staying?"

I couldn't help but notice the hope in Cass's eyes.

"For now." I lightly touched Cass's chest. "Someone needs to be around to keep an eye on you."

Cass leaned forward and kissed me quickly on the lips. "You can keep an eye on me for as long as you'd like." He grabbed my hand and stood up from his sitting position. Paisley arrived, eager to share with us the contents of her haul for the evening.

For the first time in a long time, things felt right. I mean really, really right. I still couldn't explain my need to flee when I was eighteen. I supposed Cass, and my growing feelings for him might have had something to do with it. But deep in my heart, I knew that Foxtail Lake was where I was meant to be, despite the risk of losing my heart, which was the one thing I'd vowed never to do.

I'd struggled my whole life with the family curse. I'd tried to scientifically determine if it was real or simply a fantasy born in anger and nurtured through the generations. I knew Gracie believed in it strongly, and I suspected, based on her actions, that my mom had not. If I were honest, I guess I did believe to an extent that it was her lack of belief in the curse that had led to her death, as well as the death of my father. In the end, I supposed that because the existence of a curse, or the lack thereof, could never be proven, it was best to act with caution. I liked Cass. I probably even loved him. But somewhere along the line, I'd vowed the Hollister family curse would end with me, and that was a vow I didn't take lightly.

NEXT FROM KATHI DALEY BOOKS

PREVIEW

"Oh, I don't know, Tess," Doctor Brady Baker said as we stood side by side, looking at the dilapidated old house that hadn't been lived in since before I was born. "I know I said that I liked your idea to sponsor a haunted house as a fundraiser for the animal shelter, but I wasn't necessarily thinking of using a real haunted house."

I glanced at the town's veterinarian, animal shelter owner, and all-around nice guy, who was frowning so hard he'd created a crater in the center of his forehead. "The house isn't really haunted," I assured him in a tone I hoped conveyed confidence. "At least I don't think it is." I amended, realizing that, in the end, it was probably best to be perfectly honest. "There was that one event a while back, but I'm sure the whole thing can be explained by using a rational and scientific explanation."

"What event?" Brandy asked, with a look of suspicion in his eye.

I remained silent, hoping he'd just drop it.

"You said there was that one event. What event?" he asked again.

I took Brady by the arm and walked him toward the rusty front gate which served as access the property. "It was no big deal. Really. You know how rumors get started." I rolled my eyes and huffed out a short breath that was meant to be a laugh of indifference, but sort of came out as a laugh of panic. "Everything is going to be fine, and this event is going to be spectacular, you have a Tess Thomas seal of assurance on that."

"What event, Tess?" Brady asked, digging his heels in at the gate.

I hemmed and hawed, but eventually answered. "Well, there was this one tiny incident a few years ago."

"Incident?"

I crossed my fingers behind my back to nullify the tiny white lie I was about to tell. "It really wasn't a big deal. Sure, it made the news, and there was a short investigation, but if you ask me, the whole thing was blown way out of proportion."

"What whole thing?"

"This guy from out of state bought the house and planned to open a bed and breakfast, but apparently, there was some sort of problem with the electrical. The lights kept flickering on and off, and the kitchen appliances went all wonky. The guy tried to fix the problem himself rather than calling in an electrician, but I guess he didn't know what he was doing because something happened and he was electrocuted. The estate was sold after the man who was electrocuted died, and the guy who currently owns the estate has assured me that the electrical has been dealt with, but not to worry, I plan to call in an actual electrician to fix any remaining electrical problems." I paused, smiled, and then continued. "It's a good deal, Brady. The new owner has plans to sell the place this summer after he has time to give the house a facelift, but I told him about the expansion we planned for the shelter, and he agreed to let us use the place for our fundraiser free of costs."

"Free of costs?"

I took Brady's hand and pulled him through the gate. "There are a few minor repairs that will need to be seen to, and I told him I would take care of those repairs, but I can get volunteers to help out with that. I have folks who will donate supplies and others who will donate labor if it means the shelter can be expanded to include a state of the art dog training facility and long term residential care for senior animals and difficult to place pets. White Eagle, Montana, is a town that cares about its citizens, even its four-legged citizens. I have no doubt if we sponsor this haunted house, folks will come. A lot of them. It really is a good plan."

Brady looked somewhat dazed as he stared at the house. It had been abandoned decades ago and needed more than just a few repairs to make it livable, but we didn't want to live in it. We only wanted to borrow it. I'd had a contractor look at it and had been assured that the house had good bones and was structurally sound. Yes, there were items we would need to address before we could use it to host a public event, but I hadn't been exaggerating or lying when I said I had volunteers to see to that. Of all the old houses in the area, this house, with its creepy and unusual exterior and large plot of land, was the perfect place to create our haunted house.

"So what do you think?" I asked.

"It does look as if it could really be haunted."

"It does if you believe in ghosts." I looked at Brady. "Do you believe in ghosts?"

"Not really."

"Me neither," I said even though I knew that there had been ghost sightings in the past and there were those odd noises that I'd heard when my boyfriend, Tony Marconi, and I drove out a few nights ago to get a feel for how the place would look under the moonlight. Still, even if the place was haunted, I figured we could deal with that. The reality was the crumbling exterior, interesting clock tower, dark and brooding widow's walk, and shuttered windows were absolutely perfect for what I had planned. "The large flat area to the left is going to be the graveyard," I explained, as I steadfastly pulled Brady along behind me.

"Graveyard?"

Geez, the guy really was stunned. Hadn't he ever seen a house that may or may not be haunted before?

I nodded and grinned, barely able to contain my enthusiasm. "It's an additional fundraiser. Tony is going to make a bunch of wooden headstones that people can buy and inscribe with a short epitaph. We'll place them in the cemetery, and everyone who comes out for the haunted house tour will be able to read them while they wait in line."

"Line?"

"Yes, line. If we use this house for our haunted house, I guarantee you that folks will come all the way from Billings to see it."

Brady frowned. "Billings? Doesn't Billings have their own haunted house event?"

"Well sure, but they just use an old warehouse. Their haunted house doesn't come with a legend the way ours will."

He lifted a brow. "Legend?"

Oops. I probably shouldn't have used the word legend. "You know how it is with small towns and their old houses. They all seem to have a legend." I hoped I pulled off the cheery *no need to worry* tone I was going for.

"And what might the legend of this house be?" Brady asked.

I looped my arm through his. "Oh, we don't need to talk about that right now. Let's go inside."

"What legend, Tess?"

I huffed out yet another breath. I'd expected that Brady would need to be persuaded that the house was perfect for our event, but this was turning out to be a lot more work than I'd anticipated. "I guess there may or may not have been an old cemetery on this plot of land before the house was built, and I suppose there may or may not be those who believe the souls whose resting places were disturbed currently haunt the place."

He frowned. "Why would anyone build a house on top of a cemetery?"

I giggled nervously. "Oh, you know how it is. The cemetery hadn't been used since the gold rush and land in this area is expensive. I guess what it comes down to is that everyone is looking for a bargain, and a plot of land that was used as a cemetery a century earlier, presented a bargain to the man who built the house all those years ago."

"So someone actually built a house on top of peoples' graves?"

"No, silly." I playfully swatted at Brady's shoulder. "The remains of those who'd been buried on the land were moved to another location. Now, back to our fundraiser. I think once you see the interior, you are going to love this place as much as I do." I leaned forward and really put my weight into dragging this tall man, who had to weigh double what I did, the rest of the way down the walk.

"Okay, wait." Brady froze at the threshold to the front door. "Are you actually telling me that you want to hold our shelter fundraiser in a house built on land that was previously used to house a cemetery?"

I nodded.

"Are you crazy?"

"Do you want a state of the art training facility?"

"Well, yes."

"And do you want to have a place to offer permanent housing for elderly and hard to place dogs and cats?"

"You know that I do."

"And if you were the sort who was willing to pay, say twenty bucks, to walk through a haunted house, would you be more likely to fork over the big bucks to walk through the cafeteria at the high school or a real house that folks already say is haunted?"

Both Brady's brows shot up. "You think people will pay twenty bucks to walk through a haunted house?"

"I think they will pay twenty bucks to walk through *this* haunted house." I took in a long breath, held it, and then exhaled. "Look. I'm not thrilled that the guy who built this house more than a century ago built his home on land that should have been preserved as hallowed ground. And I'm not happy that the remains of those buried on that same plot of land a century before were moved. But things were looked at differently back then and not using this house as a fundraiser isn't going to undo any of that.

It makes no sense to pass on the opportunity to raise the money we need to expand our ability to help homeless pets in the area."

Brady took a step back. He looked up at the tall structure in front of him. "Are you sure it is safe? As you just pointed out, this house is over a century old, and I know it hasn't been lived in for decades."

"I promise you that it will be safe once Tony and his band of elves get done with the place. Mike has even arranged for the county inspector to give it the green light before we begin decorating for the event."

Mike Thomas was my brother and a local police officer.

"And you think people will actually come from as far away as Billings to see the place?"

"I think droves of people will come out to see the place once *Haunted America* airs."

Brady turned and looked at me. "*Haunted America*?"

"TV show. Super popular. I know a guy who knows a guy who made the arrangements."

Brady froze. When he did not speak or move for more than fifteen seconds, I was afraid I'd shorted out the poor guy's brain.

"Look," I continued in my most persuasive voice. "I know this is a little out of the box for a fundraiser, but it is October, and everyone is into the spooky vibe. The plans we discussed for the expansion to the shelter are huge, which means that even with the large donation Tony has already made, we still need a huge fundraiser to afford to do them. A kiddie carnival or pet parade is not going to cut it. We need to go big, and a real haunted house which will be featured on *Haunted America* just about the same time our haunted house opens is exactly the sort of fundraiser that is going to get us to where we need to be. So what do you think? Are you going to go big or are you going to be the guy who passed up the chance to do something amazing?"

Brady hesitated.

"Come on, Brady. Take a chance. For the animals. For the town."

"Okay. I'm really not sure about this, but I guess we're going to go big." Brady put his hand on the doorknob. He gave it a twist and pushed the door open. I was glad I'd come by and unlocked it earlier or our dramatic moment might have been ruined. He took a step into the entry and froze. His mouth dropped open as he looked around at the large space. "Are you sure it isn't going to cost more to make this place usable than we are going to make in ticket sales?"

"I'm sure. Do you want to see the second story?"

Seconds after I asked my question, there was a crash overhead.

"Uh, thanks, but I think I'm good." Brady took a step back toward the still open door. "You've never steered me wrong in the past, and I have no reason to think you would steer me wrong now, so I guess I'll get busy on a press release letting everyone know that the White Eagle Animal Shelter is going to throw one heck of a fundraiser this year."

Books by Kathi Daley
Come for the murder, stay for the romance

Zoe Donovan Cozy Mystery:
Halloween Hijinks
The Trouble With Turkeys
Christmas Crazy
Cupid's Curse
Big Bunny Bump-off
Beach Blanket Barbie
Maui Madness
Derby Divas
Haunted Hamlet
Turkeys, Tuxes, and Tabbies
Christmas Cozy
Alaskan Alliance
Matrimony Meltdown
Soul Surrender
Heavenly Honeymoon
Hopscotch Homicide
Ghostly Graveyard
Santa Sleuth
Shamrock Shenanigans
Kitten Kaboodle
Costume Catastrophe
Candy Cane Caper
Holiday Hangover
Easter Escapade
Camp Carter
Trick or Treason
Reindeer Roundup
Hippity Hoppity Homicide

Firework Fiasco
Henderson House
Holiday Hostage
Lunacy Lake
Celtic Christmas – *December 2019*

Zimmerman Academy The New Normal
Zimmerman Academy New Beginnings
Ashton Falls Cozy Cookbook

Tj Jensen Paradise Lake Mystery:

Pumpkins in Paradise
Snowmen in Paradise
Bikinis in Paradise
Christmas in Paradise
Puppies in Paradise
Halloween in Paradise
Treasure in Paradise
Fireworks in Paradise
Beaches in Paradise
Thanksgiving in Paradise – *October 2019*

Whales and Tails Cozy Mystery:

Romeow and Juliet
The Mad Catter
Grimm's Furry Tail
Much Ado About Felines
Legend of Tabby Hollow
Cat of Christmas Past
A Tale of Two Tabbies
The Great Catsby
Count Catula
The Cat of Christmas Present

A Winter's Tail
The Taming of the Tabby
Frankencat
The Cat of Christmas Future
Farewell to Felines
A Whisker in Time
The Catsgiving Feast
A Whale of a Tail
The Catnap Before Christmas – *October 2019*

Writers' Retreat Mystery:
First Case
Second Look
Third Strike
Fourth Victim
Fifth Night
Sixth Cabin
Seventh Chapter
Eighth Witness
Ninth Grave

Rescue Alaska Mystery:
Finding Justice
Finding Answers
Finding Courage
Finding Christmas
Finding Shelter – *Early 2020*

A Tess and Tilly Mystery:

The Christmas Letter
The Valentine Mystery
The Mother's Day Mishap
The Halloween House
The Thanksgiving Trip
The Saint Paddy's Promise
The Halloween Haunting – *September 2019*

The Inn at Holiday Bay:

Boxes in the Basement
Letters in the Library
Message in the Mantel
Answers in the Attic
Haunting in the Hallway
Pilgrim in the Parlor – *October 2019*
Note in the Nutcracker – *December 2019*

A Cat in the Attic Mystery:

The Curse of Hollister House
The Mystery Before Christmas – *November 2019*

The Hathaway Sisters:

Harper
Harlow
Hayden – *Early 2020*

Haunting by the Sea:

Homecoming by the Sea
Secrets by the Sea
Missing by the Sea
Betrayal by the Sea
Thanksgiving by the Sea – *October 2019*

Sand and Sea Hawaiian Mystery:

Murder at Dolphin Bay
Murder at Sunrise Beach
Murder at the Witching Hour
Murder at Christmas
Murder at Turtle Cove
Murder at Water's Edge
Murder at Midnight
Murder at Pope Investigations

Seacliff High Mystery:

The Secret
The Curse
The Relic
The Conspiracy
The Grudge
The Shadow
The Haunting

Road to Christmas Romance:

Road to Christmas Past

USA Today best-selling author Kathi Daley lives in beautiful Lake Tahoe with her husband Ken. When she isn't writing, she likes spending time hiking the miles of desolate trails surrounding her home. She has authored more than a hundred books in twelve series. Find out more about her books at www.kathidaley.com

Stay up-to-date:
Newsletter, *The Daley Weekly* http://eepurl.com/NRPDf
Webpage – www.kathidaley.com
Facebook at Kathi Daley Books – www.facebook.com/kathidaleybooks
Kathi Daley Books Group Page – https://www.facebook.com/groups/569578823146850/
E-mail – kathidaley@kathidaley.com
Twitter at Kathi Daley@kathidaley – https://twitter.com/kathidaley
Amazon Author Page – https://www.amazon.com/author/kathidaley
BookBub – https://www.bookbub.com/authors/kathi-daley

52847965R00131

Made in the USA
Lexington, KY
24 September 2019